BOOK 5

# GHOST HUNTRESS the discovery

## MARLEY GIBSON

GRAPHIA

Houghton Mifflin Harcourt
Boston   New York   2011

www.hmhbooks.com

The text of this book is set in Bembo.

Library of Congress Cataloging-in-Publication Data
Gibson, Marley.
The discovery / by Marley Gibson.
p. cm.—(Ghost huntress)
Summary: While awaiting DNA test results that could determine the identity of her
biological father, high-school senior Kendall Moorehead and her friends use their psychic
abilities against an evil, Civil War-era doll said to have been made by a voodoo priestess.
[1. Psychic ability—Fiction. 2. Ghosts—Fiction. 3. Dolls—Fiction. 4. Voodoo—Fiction.
5. Identity—Fiction. 6. Georgia—Fiction.] I. Title.
PZ7.G345Dis 2011
[Fic]—dc22
2010039249

ISBN: 978-0-547-39308-7

Manufactured in the United States of America
DOM 10 9 8 7 6 5 4 3 2 1
4500285630

# ACKNOWLEDGMENTS

To all the places where I wrote this book:

1. In the rig ... my wonderful home on wheels
2. In Gettysburg, an amazing town filled with history ... and ghosts
3. In Champion, Pennsylvania ... no Internet access, but that gave me more time to write
4. In Standish, Michigan ... again, no Internet, so a gal's gotta write
5. In the car ... as my sweetheart drove us through the Upper Peninsula of Michigan and over into Wisconsin and the Dells, where I managed some water-sliding time
6. At Rachel Heggaton and Chris Fleming's house ... thanks for the hospitality, the breakfast in bed, and the awesome time at the Buffett concert
7. At John and Ann Burns's house ... thanks for letting me take over your dining room table for a couple of weeks. Twenty-five days—phew!

And—

To Patrick Burns, for his amazing love and support and for saving my computer as it was trying to die on me. And to the kidlets, William and Alec, for an amazing summer

To Julia Richardson, for giving me *one* more day—after the Fourth of July—to reread and perfect the story. No more deadlines during major holidays! LOL!

To Deidre Knight, for always believing in me and taking care of me

To those who have empowered me through gifting hardships for me to overcome, inadvertently challenging me to be a stronger person and conquer anything

To my family, for their continued support

To ShoulderHill Films, for trying to get Kendall and the gang on the big screen

To all the fans who keep reading the adventures . . . hope there'll be more!

*To the woman who taught me the love and appreciation of words
and how to use my imagination to create anything;
an English teacher, a world-class musician,
and the role model of a lifetime:
my mother, Elizabeth Ann Marley Harbuck*

*The boundaries which divide Life from Death*
*are at best shadowy and vague.*
*Who shall say where the one ends,*
*and where the other begins?*

*—Edgar Allan Poe*

# CHAPTER ONE

I'M ABOUT TO WALK INTO A STRANGER'S place of business, introduce myself, and ask the million-dollar question of my life: *Do you know who my father is?*

How freakin' messed up is that?

I take a deep breath and slowly let out the pent-up air through my parted lips, allowing my lungs to stretch and contract like a taut rubber band. Maybe that's the tightness I'm feeling in my chest. Yeah, right . . . couldn't be the fact that I'm in St. Louis in search of someone who might know what man contributed the DNA that eventually became Kendall Moorehead.

Mom—my adopted mom, Sarah Moorehead—reaches over and rubs her hand on my jeaned kneecap. "We're here, sweetie. We can do this."

I nod when I really want to shake my head back and forth and totally chicken out on this expedition. Stealing a look in the visor mirror, I check for mascara flakes or food in my teeth from the cookies I had on the plane from Atlanta. All clear. Makeup . . . good. Clothes . . . mostly unwrinkled. Hair . . .

pulled away from face with a sparkly clip, brushed, and wavy. I'm as ready to go as I can possibly be.

Mom puts her purse strap over her shoulder and fists the rental-car keys in her palm. I climb out and listen as the automatic locks click shut.

I squint into the Saturday-afternoon sunshine and glance at the gold-trimmed glass sign in front of the quaint art gallery on Twelfth Street here in downtown St. Louis. It reads ANDREA CAMINITI STUDIO.

See, here's the current sitch: I just got back from my Enlightened Youth Retreat in California, where I met my new boyfriend, Patrick Lynn (who's psychic just like me), and I told the parentals about the vision I had about the person who may or may not be my biological father. My bestie, Celia Nichols, dug up information on the name that I saw in my vision: Andy Caminiti. Actually, the name was Andi Caminiti. So, either my real dad had a sex change (eww!) or I'm about to meet a member of his immediate family.

My psychic awareness tells me it's the latter.

"Let's go, Kendall," Mom says. She leads the way across the sidewalk and through the double-glass doors of the art gallery.

My nostrils pick up the smell of turpentine, oil paint, and scented candles. Canvases adorn the left wall, laser whips of splashed colors in abstract patterns. To the right are more traditional artsy pieces of rolling hills, sunsets, beaches, and landscapes done in charcoal and watercolors. A spiral staircase in the middle leads upward to a wide-open loft area that I can see is full of black-and-white photographs of people. Close-ups of eyes, mouths, arms, and . . . is that a picture of a bellybutton? Weird . . . yet beautifully shot.

For a moment, I consider this woman, Andi Caminiti, who is quite well known in the art community of St. Louis, Missouri, and I wonder how in the world I could possibly be related to such a talented person. I can barely draw stick figures.

A young girl with tight curls and fashionable black glasses greets us.

"Welcome to Andrea Caminiti's gallery," she says. "I'm Liza. May I show you around?"

Mom gently clears her throat. "Thank you, Liza, but we have an appointment."

Liza adjusts her glasses on her plump face. "You must be Mrs. Moorehead. Andi will be right down to see you. Have a seat and I'll get you some bottled water while you wait."

We smile and move behind Liza over to an area where two white-leather couches sit facing each other. When I came home from California and told Mom and Dad all about my psychic visions and the connection to the name in St. Louis, my 'rents didn't hesitate to go online and book two tickets out here to St. Louis for this Saturday morning. Mom called ahead to the gallery on the pretext of wanting to purchase some of the artist's work for our new house . . . so here we are.

Liza holds out two cold, plastic bottles. "Sparkling or still?"

"Still, thanks."

I take the proffered drink, twist off the cap, and quickly

douse the fiery burn in my throat. How am I going to do this? Do I have the guts to reveal what I know to a total stranger? Will she be nice? Mean? Will she kick us out, or, worse, call the police and have them put us in the loony bin? Do we even still have loony bins in this country? These thoughts—who needs them?

My BlackBerry vibrates in my pocket, and I draw it out. Patrick is texting me. Of course he is. We're cosmically connected.

>Clam down. Everything will work out. P

I love how our brains and psyches are linked, even four states apart.

The tapping of three-inch heels on the wooden spiral staircase causes me to jerk my head up. I see her legs first. Long and lean, like a runner. A flowy black skirt then comes into view followed by a loose-fitting black chiffon top. From the back, the woman is tall and thin with jet-black hair. As she turns, her ivory face is highlighted by bright red lipstick and lush black lashes surrounding her … hazel eyes. Wow—they're sort of the same color as mine.

"Sarah?" she asks as she walks toward us with her right hand extended. "I'm Andi. So nice of you to come all this way to see my work."

Mom and I both stand and the adults exchange handshakes. I literally stare at the pretty lady in front of me, wondering how I'm going to start this convo. My throat becomes as arid as the California desert I flew over on the way home from my retreat. My eyes begin to water and I'm afraid that if I blink, it'll look like I'm crying. A stabbing pain cranks over my left eyebrow and I suddenly feel like I've been here before. Vuja de of another time. Been here, met her before. I don't know why my psychic senses pick this exact moment to get all wibble-tated. New word Patrick taught me; he picked it up from kids at his previous school, in Tampa. Meaning "distorted." And I think that totally defines my life these days.

Eyes that mirror my own turn to me, and Mom makes the introduction.

"This is my daughter Kendall. Thank you for taking the time to meet us."

"Pleased to meet you both," Andi says.

My hand slides into Andi's delicate one and I suddenly see flashes of her as a child. Long black hair gathered in a ponytail that's being pulled by a nearly identical twin. Only he's a he. Andy. Andy Caminiti. The name I envisioned. The two children are laughing and playing and wrestling over a go-cart. I pull my hand back, not wanting to invade memories of a family I may or may not be a part of.

Andi takes in my sudden action but smiles. "Have you had a chance to look around the gallery?"

"Not really, but it seems pretty cool to have your own gallery," I say.

"It is," she says. "Took me a while, but here I am." She pauses. "Are you an artist, Kendall?"

The laughter bubbles out before I can stop it. "No, ma'am. Crayolas were never my friend."

Mom sets her hand on my shoulder. "Kendall's talents lie in other areas." She stops a moment and I know she's going to get this picnic rolling. "Perhaps we can sit somewhere more private so we can discuss . . . things."

Andi's bright red smile widens. "Certainly. Come up to my office and we can talk about your decorating needs and if you want something photographic for your space or something on a canvas."

I feel sort of bad that we're leading this nice lady on, but it's what we have to do.

After fifteen minutes of touring the upstairs photo gallery and then flipping through Andi's portfolio in her office, I can't take it anymore. The intense stabbing pain over my eyebrow is a reminder of my mission here.

"You have very lovely work, Andi," Mom says. "I think that black-and-white photo of the St. Louis arch would look lovely in—"

I stop her with my hand on her arm. "Mom."

She lifts her eyes to mine and then licks her lips nervously. She knows I'm ready.

"Ms. Caminiti," I start.

"Andi, please."

I repeat the name I've said a thousand times in my head. "Andi. Thanks." I swallow hard through the daggered dryness. I can do this. "Andi, your artwork is totally gorgeous, but there's another reason that Mom and I came all this way to talk to you."

She sits back and then laces her fingers together in her lap. "Go ahead."

"You see . . . umm . . . like, I'm adopted. My birth mother was . . . Emily Jane Faulkner."

Psychic abilities aren't needed to read Andi Caminiti's reaction. The name is not foreign to her. "I see."

"Do you?" I ask pointedly. "You know that name?"

She shrugs, very noncommittal.

I push forward. "I'm the daughter of Emily Jane Faulkner and, perhaps, of your brother, Andy Caminiti. They dated in college and both disappeared seventeen years ago. Neither has been heard from since."

Andi pushes out of her chair and strides over to the window. Her eyes stare out ahead through the pane as her index finger rests between her teeth. "It's widely known that my twin brother disappeared many years ago. What exactly do you want, Miss Moorehead?"

My brief stint in studying auras and the bit I learned from my roomie at the retreat, Jessica Spencer, tells me that Andrea Caminiti is six kinds of pissed off at me at this moment. The vibrant red that radiates off her head tells me of her fear and strong anxiety. Wisps of black float through the red aura. From what I learned from Jess, this means hatred, negativity, depression. My heart hurts for the pain I must be causing Andi with this conversation. I can't blame her for being greatly irritated with me. Some stranger shows up wanting to buy her art, and then the convo turns to something personal and painful.

I too stand. "I just want you to listen. I've psychically seen your brother and Emily in the burning car wreck that took their lives seventeen years ago. I believe that Andy died that night, and had it not been for the paramedics that got Emily out of the car and to the hospital—where my mom was an emergency-room nurse—I would have died too."

I give her a moment as I watch her eyes grow wide.

My pulse trills under my skin. "I'm psychic, and my visions have brought me to you. I've seen your name and I've been led here to find my family."

The woman isn't having any of this. It's at this moment that I wish I'd opted for the speech-communication class this semester so I'd know exactly what to say and how to show the proper body language to calm her unease. This is certainly not the most fluid exchange I've ever had.

The once friendly and welcoming hazel eyes turn blazingly hella-bad on me. "Do you know how many psychics have walked through my door telling me they know where my brother is or what happened to him?"

"No, I just—"

"Dozens! Literally dozens of them! They've told me everything from Andy's being a victim of a serial killer to his joining the merchant marines and sailing off to Asia to his being involved in the slave trade. I've had psychics tell me his soul was in my dog, represented in my artwork, and, best of all, living in an old bottle of sand that I have in my house that he and I collected together in Myrtle Beach when we were eleven. Do you know how many of these psychics' stories I've hung my hat on, only to be vastly disappointed in the end when I still have no clue where he is or what happened to him?"

She stops her tirade to drink in air, and I take the opportunity to try to bring calm, if that's even possible. "Yes, ma'am. I totally understand. I've struggled with this whole psychic awakening like you wouldn't believe. But I've been right about so many things. And my visions brought me to the fact that Emily Jane Faulkner *was* my birth mother. She *did* date your brother in college, didn't she?"

"That's none of your business," Andi snaps. I've hit a nerve.

"It is, though," I say, nearly begging. "I'm trying to find out *who* I am. You are a missing piece of the puzzle."

"That's not my problem, young lady."

Mom tries to intervene. "Andi, if you'd just—"

She spins on her high heels. "Just what? Have hope? Mrs. Moorehead, I've spent the last seventeen years trying to come to terms with my brother's disappearance. My twin brother. The person I shared a womb with. The person who was the only sibling I had. The person who was my best friend. I've been down this road before." Andi's eyes connect with mine again and then shift back to Mom. "This is an original act, I'll admit. Pimping your daughter out as a psychic so I'll react differently. That's rich."

I flatten my lips. "It's not an act, Andi."

"Who are you to suddenly come out of the woodwork?" Andi asks. The curls of black in her aura strengthen. "What do you want? A piece of the family fortune? You think that coming in here and saying you're my missing, perhaps dead, brother's long-lost child will entitle you to some sort of inheritance?"

*What?* "Umm . . . *no*. What money? Who cares about money? I just want to know who I am. Anything that might explain why I'm psychic and where I came from."

Mom steps between Andi and me. "We apologize, Ms. Caminiti, for any hurt or confusion we've caused. You have to understand that I'll do anything for my daughter. Believe me, I doubted her abilities as well, but she's the real deal."

Andi crosses her slim arms over her middle. "That's what they all say. I'd be much obliged if you two would just leave now. I'll forget this discussion ever took place."

Now tears do threaten, stinging at the back of my eyes. I *know* I'm connected to this woman. It's so clear; it's like gazing in a mirror and seeing my face looking back at me. "I *don't* want you to forget this visit happened. I want you to remember. I want you to think about any details of your brother's life. I want you to think of me."

She hangs her head and her silky black hair surrounds her face. A soft, emotionally choked voice says, "Please show yourself out. I have work to do."

I stretch my fingers to reach out to Andi, stopping only inches away from her. Flashed pictures dance through my head of Andi and me laughing together in the future, hugging even. We *are* meant to be in each other's lives.

My hand drops to my side and I muster up the courage to

say one last thing. "I'm willing to submit to DNA testing to see if we're related. Anything to know who I am and where I came from. No strings attached."

The words hang in the air like drying laundry.

She scoffs and then extends her hand to indicate the spiral staircase. Mom tugs on mine and we descend to the main level. Surprisingly enough, Andi follows; the clicking of her heels taps out her judgment.

I stop and turn. "Please?"

Our similar hazel eyes lock and I sense a light of hope in the irises. It's brief, but it's there. So I reach into my purse and pull out the index card I'd filled out earlier, in the rental car. The one with my name, address, cell phone number, e-mail addy, Mom's cell, and the landline at our house in Radisson. I give the neatly written information to Andi Caminiti and take her hand in mine. Her warmth spreads to me, and I feel that there's a chance.

"Can we just try?"

# CHAPTER TWO

IN RADISSON, IT'S TIME TO GET BACK into the groove of my life—whatever that may be now—and not think about the encounter with Andi Caminiti or if I'll ever hear from her again.

The ball is in her court at this point, so I just need to focus on my friends, family, Patrick, and school. Bleck ... and I really have to hunker down in history class. Mr. Rorek isn't concerned about what's happening in my present. He wants me only to focus on the past and write a paper that will impress him.

Monday at lunch, I sit with Celia, Becca, and Shelby-Nichole, and we talk about our ghost hunting. Since the departure of Taylor Tillson to Alaska—with He Who Shall Not Be Mentioned, aka Jason "Won't Message or E-mail Me" Tillson—Shelby-Nichole has taken over as resident photographer for our group. It's great to have her with us, but I'll admit that her photography isn't as keen as Taylor's. That girl has a psychic eye for capturing the most amazing pictures.

This is good.

I need this.

Back to life. Back to reality.

Back to ghost hunting. I want to use the skills that I developed at the retreat in California to really help with cases and do more to help families who have experienced not only paranormal activity but also possibly fear and loss. Like what I'm trying to do with Andi Caminiti. No, no, no . . . I won't think about her right now. Or my potential father. I'll listen to Celia as she reviews possible cases for us.

"Oh, you'll love this one. We've gotten an e-mail from this guy in Savannah who insists that he has a 'haunted sandwich' in his house," she reports with a straight face. Nothing rattles Celia Nichols. Doesn't miss a beat on the weird, outrageous, and wicked bizarre.

"Get out of town," Becca says with a laugh.

"A haunted sandwich?" I ask. "Is that even possible?"

Celia flips through her ghost-huntress notepad. "One James Pendergrass reports that he made a ham sandwich for his son, Jeffrey, age seven, two weeks ago, and before his son could eat it, a Civil War soldier came up out of the floor in his kitchen and went into the sandwich. Mr. Pendergrass claims that this turned the sandwich into a ghost and it's now haunting him."

Becca twists her black-dyed hair around her index finger. "What's this guy been smoking and why ain't he sharing?" she says, tongue-in-cheek.

I hold up my hand to stop everyone. "May I suggest we move on to a more sane case?" I just can't deal with someone *that* wack right now.

Celia moves to the next note. "Okay, there's a huge historical

display that's going to be at the Radisson fairgrounds this weekend, focusing on the town's haunted past. It's this exhibit of
objects from an old house in town that no one goes into. Imagine getting your hands on some of those historical items. I was
thinking we could go together and maybe try our hand at getting some EVPs from the old relics?"

"I'm cool with that," Becca says. "I have a new recorder I
want to test out."

"And, Kendall," Celia says, "you can try your hand at psychometry."

"What's that?" Shelby-Nichole asks.

Before I can answer, Celia speaks up. "Psychometry is the
ability to draw out information about people, events, health,
career, whatever is associated with an object, just by touching
it or being near it."

"That's pretty cool," Shelby-Nichole says. She turns to me.
"And you can do that?"

I nod. "What kind of items are in the display?"

"Pots, pans, clothing from the Civil War," Celia notes.
"Some musket balls, clapboard and such from houses, pictures,
tintypes, and, oh . . . then there's Xander the Doll, who I've
been dying to see. They don't let him out much."

"Xander the what?" Becca asks with a brow raised.

Celia almost pants with excitement. "Xander the Doll is
like from the late eighteen hundreds and has all sorts of curses
and stories attached to him. When he was still owned by the
Farnsworth family the neighbors always cliamed he was re-

sponsible for weird shit that happened. Like lamps breaking, slats falling out of beds, that kind of thing. Worse stuff too, like sickness and bad injuries. Back then people said it was Xander that wreaked all the havoc."

"A doll?" Becca asks flatly. "Yeah, right. I've heard some stories, Nichols, but that one takes the cake."

Shaking her short black bob, Celia presses her lips together. "It's Radisson history. I remember hearing about it when I was a little kid."

"Where's the doll been?" I ask.

Celia shrugs and continues. "I haven't heard anything about Xander the Doll in forever. So it's going to be amazing to see him in the historical collection." She turns to me. "You're totally going to connect with him."

"Works for me." I can kill two birds with one stone: work on my psychometry skills and research Radisson's history to help me out with my Civil War paper. After all, it's not going to write itself.

The bell rings for fifth period so we gather up our lunch trays and clear out.

I wave to my *chicas* and then rush to my locker to grab my history book.

As I'm clicking the lock back in place, a text comes in.

>Trig class boring. Thinking of u.

>Just finished lunch. Thinking of u 2.

>c u Friday afternoon.

>Long wait. 2 long.

>Ditto that.

>Skype after school?

>Of course. Enjoy history.

>TTYL!

Awww ... Patrick's so awesome. Imagine that—a boyfriend who actually texts! Oh, did I go there? Yep. I did. Sorry, but I'm still a little bitter over how Jason Tillson and I were like all in love and stuff and then he just—*poof*—disappeared from my life like he was never there. Yeah, yeah, he had to move to his dad's in Alaska, but the last I checked, they did have cell phones and e-mail and Internet connections there. Haven't heard diddly-squat from him since we said goodbye in his driveway.

But Patrick ...

*Happy sigh.*

He came along at just the right time and to just the right place. For both of us, actually.

Well, we thought we were going to have to do the long-distance-relationship thing, but the hand of fate stepped in and the air force transferred his father to the Atlanta area. Now, Patrick and his dad live in this nice house in Duluth, Georgia, which is only a forty-five-minute drive from Radisson.

*He* calls me all the time. *He* texts me all the time. My Facebook profile is a picture of the two of us all smashy-faced together; he stretched out his arm and took the picture with his cell phone. Not that I'm worrying about it or anything, but I can't help wondering if Jason's checked out my page all the way up there in Alaska. I mean, everyone comments on how perfect Patrick and I are together. And I have to agree. Patrick and I mesh so much better than Jason and I did. Not that I didn't like being with Jason. It's just that Patrick and I share this psychic connection. He's not too overprotective of me or cynical about my abilities. He gets why I have to use my skills, investigate, and try to help people. Patrick appreciates what it's like to see, hear, and feel things that you can't explain. He understands the voices and visions in my head because he has them himself. We sometimes share them, in fact.

Now I dreamily float down the hallway toward the door that reads Mr. Scotty Rorek, my history teacher. I take my seat in the third row, plant my elbows on top of the desk, and rest my chin in my hands. Closing my eyes, I conjure up Patrick's handsome face, drawing it in my mind from memory. That firm jaw. Those chocolate brown eyes. The handful of gray hair at his temples. And the tat on his arm that is just like the one I have. Little bugger still stings like crazy and it's a task hiding it from my mom. She will go totally ballistic when she sees it, if she ever does.

Mr. Rorek walks in and sets his gigamonic coffee mug on the podium. "Turn to chapter twelve and let's talk about the Battle of Gettysburg, a pivotal moment in the War Between the States that some say . . ."

I tune Mr. Rorek out a bit as I think about Patrick and getting to know him better. Jason and I rushed things so much in our relationship. Patrick and I don't feel like we're on some sort of deadline. With Jason, I was the new girl in town with this strange ability and we were thrown together. That whole opposites-attracting thing. It was like wham, bam, it's over, ma'am. Just when I fell hard for Jason, everything blew up in our faces. And my heart truly broke when we said goodbye. I didn't have to be psychic to know that a long-distance Georgia-to-Alaska relationship wasn't going to work. I just never imagined it would be a cold-turkey thing.

Even though Patrick lives in another town, we've got it all worked out to hang as often as possible. We Skype for hours at a time—even helping each other with our respective home-work—and he plans on coming to Radisson every weekend to hang out, ghost hunt with the girls and me. And, of course, some quality one-on-one time. Father Mass has an extra bedroom at the rectory, so Patrick has a home away from home. I do believe I'm settling into this psychic existence, my abilities, and all the new people in my life.

"Earth to Kendall. Come in, Kendall," Mr. Rorek shouts.

Bolting upright, I look to the front of the class. "Yes, sir?"

"I was asking if you could tell me the name of the regiment that defended Little Round Top at the battle on the second day of Gettysburg?"

"Oh." *Umm. Err.* Busted daydreaming about my life.

I'm saved, though, as my spirit guide, Anona, a beautiful Native American woman, appears next to my desk, tsk-tsking and shaking her head.

"The regiment, Kendall? You did read the assignment, right?"

"Yes, Mr. Rorek." Okay, that's a bit of a fib. I started reading last night but fell asleep. I look to Anona, begging her with my eyes for some scholarly assistance. She smiles and shows me a New England state and a number.

"It was the Twentieth Maine," I say firmly.

Mr. Rorek nods and then harrumphs. "I hope you'll pay much more attention to the Radisson Civil War display at the fairgrounds, Ms. Moorehead."

How does he know about my psychometry experiment? "Sir?"

He passes back a stack of papers giving our new assignment. I glance down and see that he's referring to the same exhibit Celia was telling us about at lunch. He says, "I'm requiring all three of my history classes to visit the notable display this weekend and answer questions on what you see. There's nothing like witnessing history for yourself." The teacher stops in front of my row and peers at me. "I assume you'll be able to accomplish that, Kendall?"

A smile creeps across my face. "You betcha!"

Awesome . . . getting a grade for ghost hunting. What could be easier?

## CHAPTER THREE

THE WEEK FLIES BY with lots of pop quizzes that make my head ache, homework assignments that make my eyes bleed, and laborious hours on the yearbook that make my hair hurt. It's like the teachers and advisers are trying to catch up on the time we "wasted" while we were away on our spring break. I mean, what did they do? Plot and plan against us? Didn't they get some beach time or chillax time too?

I couldn't be happier to see Friday roll in.

I'm home from school with barely enough time to foof my hair, brush my teeth, and dab on a little extra mascara before the front doorbell rings.

"It's Patrick!" I shout as I bound down the stairs of our hundred-plus-year-old house. This is his first trip to Radisson to meet the parentals and all my friends. Cocky boy that he is, he's not worried a bit. I guess I shouldn't be either.

"I'll get it!" Kaitlin screams out, dashing by me.

"It's for me," I insist.

"Nuh-uh, it's Penny Carmickle and Daisy Reinhart coming over!"

"Umm, Kaitlin, I'm psychic. I know it's my boyfriend."

"Which one?" she asks and then sticks her tongue out at me. All I can do is freeze in my tracks next to the piano that sits in the front hallway.

Kaitlin beats me to the door and jerks it open. I know I'm right when I see her small shoulders slump. "Oh. You must be the new one."

Patrick flashes her a dazzling smile and ignores her snarky remark. "You must be Kaitlin."

She shifts her weight to one hip. "Kennnnnnnnnndaaaaalll!"

I step in. "You're such a brat, Kaitlin. I told you it was for me." She retreats into the kitchen and I slide forward.

A timid *hi* squeaks out from me.

I haven't seen Patrick since we said goodbye to each other at the Fresno airport after our retreat. I never knew I could miss someone so much. Especially someone that I'd just met.

"I missed you too, Kendall," he says, reading my thoughts, like we can do when we're in close proximity.

And . . . I melt.

He no longer wears the knit hat, gloves, and sunglasses to shield himself from all the psychic vibes in the air around him. Oliver, the counselors, and our retreat seemed to work just fine on him. Of course, saving me from drowning in the Cream of Pacific Ocean helped us both over a big hurdle. It was at that moment that I knew he and I were destined to be together. Now, Patrick stretches his right hand out and snags my fingers, tugging me toward him. We come together in a warm embrace that has my toes literally tingling.

I drink in the smell of him. Shaving cream. Deodorant. A smidgety-bit of some tangy cologne. Nothing too icky-smelling. I find him doing the same, sniffing my hair.

"Mmm . . . you smell like blooming flowers," he says all dreamily.

"Nope. Just Neutrogena," I say with a laugh.

Patrick's eyes crinkle into a smile and he chuckles along with me. Then his face tightens into a way-serious look. OMG—he's going to kiss me!

*Yes, I am,* he says to me telepathically. *Now be quiet.*

All words, thoughts, and emotions are tossed into the air above me; they scatter like fallen leaves, then rearrange themselves and dive back into me in a pattern of pure joy, happiness, and crushdom. Patrick turns his head to the right and lowers his lips to mine. Soft and sweet at first. Then a bit more frenzied. Warm skin meeting and saying hello after a long time away from each other. We move together; our arms wrap around each other in a clinging embrace. He deepens the kiss more and nearly takes my breath away.

And I thought Jason Tillson could kiss!

*Do you really want to think about him while we're doing this?*

*I was just saying . . .*

*And I was just saying, focus on me.*

*Yes, sir.*

So much for keeping any secrets from this guy.

*Damn right.*

Somewhere overhead, I hear bells, yet I don't stop kissing Patrick until I hear a gagging sound from behind me.

"Do I have to be subjected to this again?" Kaitlin asks.

Patrick and I pull apart and he blushes from cheek to cheek. I roll my eyes at my little sister and say, "Whatever."

She opens the door to her friends Penny and Daisy and the three of them swerve off to the right to attack the Wii. I thread my fingers into Patrick's and lead him to the kitchen. I open the fridge to show him macaroni salad, a leftover breakfast frittata, and last night's fried chicken Mom made for dinner.

"Pick your poison."

"Fried chicken, please."

Just as he's finishing a second drumstick, Mom walks in the back door.

"TGIF!" she exclaims. "It seems like the stomach flu is running rampant in this town. I swear, we saw—" She stops in her tracks as she's pushing out of her sensible nurse shoes. A vivid, welcoming smile crosses her face. "*You* have to be Patrick. I'm Sarah Moorehead."

Patrick politely wipes his hands on a napkin, stands, and walks over to my mother. "Hey there, Mrs. Moorehead. Nice to meet you."

"Please, call me Sarah."

"I'll try," Patrick says with a nod.

Mom shifts her eyes to the chicken bones. "I see you kids have helped yourselves."

"Yes, ma'am," he says. "It was delicious. I haven't had a home-cooked meal in a while, so I appreciate your efforts."

"Why's that?" Mom asks with her brow raised.

Patrick stubs his sneakered foot against the base of the kitchen island. "Oh, well, you know, with Dad being in the military and all. I get a lot of chow that he brings to me from the officers club. My mom, from what I can remember, was never really much of a cook. I've pretty much grown up on Burger King and FatDonald's," he says with a laugh.

Mom rubs his shoulder. "That's a shame about your mom, sweetie. Before you head home on Sunday, I'm going to cook you an amazing homemade meal. What's your favorite dish?"

He leers my way and I read his thoughts: *Kendall.*

Now I blush from cheek to cheek. *Be good. This is my mom!*

"I love pot roast with potatoes, onions, and carrots. My grandmother used to make it for us when we lived near her in Colorado."

"Yankee pot roast it will be," Mom says like the happy homemaker she is.

I grab my purse and car keys. "I'm taking him over to Father Mass's and then we're going to the fairgrounds."

"Don't you need your history assignment?" Mom asks.

"Oh, right." I turn to Patrick. "BRB."

I fly up the stairs two at a time and rummage through the

dirty clothes on the floor to find my backpack I abandoned earlier. I lug out the assignment Mr. Rorek gave us and am about to haul ass back downstairs when Anona, my spirit guide, appears to me.

"Whoa, whoa, whoa! Anona!"

It's too late to try to be graceful. I land flat on my buttocks on a dirty pair of jeans and the Prada knockoff sandals I got at Aldo. Not exactly thrilled with my spirit guide, I roll to my right hip to rub my left cheek, which is smarting something fierce.

"What's the deal, Anona?"

Her voice is sweet and calm although her statement is chilling. "Beware of danger tonight, Kendall."

I let out a long sigh and stand up. "Can you be a little more specific?"

"Danger lurks in the darkness."

Standing face-to-face with the beautiful Native woman, I stab my fists to my hips. "A little more detail and a little less mystery would be nice. Are we talking danger like when I'm driving the car? Or staying away from the hot-dog carts? Or on one of the carnival rides?"

I've read horror stories online about these carnivals that travel from town to town. They never get all the bolts and mechanics on the rides set right. People have been flung out; they've fallen from twisty heights or tripped on loose wires, cords, and plates. Gack! Now I sound like my mom, even making the fair not fun.

Anona's eyebrows knit together in displeasure. "Heed my word. Help your friends."

"Dude, it's just the Radisson fairgrounds. What? Is someone's prize bull going to rush out from the judging area? Salmonella in the blue-ribbon blueberry pie?" I wave her off and close the door to my room, hoping just to have a nice night with Patrick and my friends. Sure, I'll have to do some homework for Mr. Rorek, but I can't wait to get on the Tilt-a-Whirl and ride the Scrambler.

At the base of the stairs, I shout out, "Let's go, Patrick!"

For me, danger always lurks everywhere. How is tonight going to be different?

We drop Patrick's duffle and car off at Father Mass's—he wasn't there; probably out with Loreen—and head straight to the fairgrounds. There are a kajillion cars in the parking lot, so I steer my Honda Fit through the grassy pathway where the guy is directing me with orange-lit cones. It looks like everyone and his brother is here tonight for the rides and festivities.

Me, if I didn't have the history assignment, I'd come just for the cotton candy. Can't get enough of the stuff.

"I've got this," Patrick says at the ticket booth. "What kind of date would it be if I made you pay?"

I waggle the history assignment at him. "I had to come anyway because of Mr. Rorek."

"Let me," he says with a smile, and then quickly kisses my lips.

*Mmm . . . mmm . . . mmm . . .*

I take the ticket from Patrick and he grasps my hand. Our fingers plait together like a French braid as he leads me into the pavilion area.

"Hey, Kendall!" Celia calls out, waving.

Clay is examining the bull behind the wooden fence like he knows what he's looking at or something.

"What up, Price?" I ask.

He nods. "Fine specimen of a Black Angus bull. You know, Angus are a Scottish breed and where we get most of our beef products from. They're naturally polled, which means they don't have horns. And his shiny black coat looks like they feed him a lot of corn and soy. You know, they also come in red, but black is the most popular in the United States, with more than—"

"Okay, okay, okay, we get it," Celia interrupts. Even the science geek rolls her eyes. "Clay, are you, like, planning on getting a degree in animal husbandry or something?"

I laugh. "Umm, hello, Dr. Kettle, Mr. Pot is here." Celia can go on for days with tidbits and *Jeopardy!*-like factoids. She and Clay are perfectly matched.

"My uncle has a farm in Alabama, okay? Can I not be interested in the animal?"

I giggle. "I'd be more interested in him if he had a strip of bacon and a slice of cheese on his back."

Celia smacks me. Then she looks at my brown-eyed, brown-haired companion. "Oh my God! It's the infamous Patrick Lynn from California!"

He flashes her a grin. "I actually live in Duluth now."

"No," Celia insists. "From the Skype when Kendall was at camp—"

"—it wasn't camp, it was—"

"—from the night I drew that missing girl for you," she concludes, totally stepping over my lines.

Patrick grins at her. "Oh! You're Celia. Awesome to finally meet you."

They shake hands in a very grown-up way and she introduces him to her boyfriend, Clay Price. "Don't mind him," Celia starts. "Ever since he dissected that pig fetus in biology, he's had this thing for animals."

"Whatever," Clay says. "Y'all want to go hit some rides?"

I wave the history assignment like a flag of surrender. "I have to check out the Radisson Civil War display first. But let's meet by the Scrambler in a little while."

"Sounds good to me," Clay says.

"I actually don't have the history stuff to do, Clay, but I'm gonna go check it out with Kendall and Patrick, okay?" Celia says.

Clay leans over and gives her a kiss on the cheek and then goes back to scrutinizing the bull.

The three of us continue walking through the pavilion. Celia is snapping pics of the dresses that Civil War–era women wore, as well as some soldier's boots and a rifle in a glass case. There are pictures of Radisson from before the war, when it was a delicately hidden Southern gem, to pictures afterward, when it was mired in Reconstruction. The cotton mill was burned and the river blockaded to prevent any goods going through.

"Wow, I had no idea that the puny river in the cemetery was once this monstrous shipping track," I say, staring at the exhibit.

"Pretty cool, huh?" Celia agrees.

Soon, we're joined by several other RHSers, all here for the same reason. Becca and Dragon are here, as are Shelby-Nichole and her boyfriend, Colton. The athletic brigade is here as well: Sean Carmickle, Jim Roach, and Kyle Kadish, with cheerleaders Courtney Langdon, Stephanie Crawford, and Farah Lewis.

"Mr. Rorek?" Stephanie asks.

I scrunch up my face. "Yup. You too?"

Farah waves her history printout. "I'm never eating pork again after the stench I just endured walking through that livestock barn. And me in my new Steve Maddens."

Celia frowns. "Pigs are actually very clean animals. It's humans' putting them in pens with mud and their own squalor that make them smell to high heaven like they do. I once read this article in *Progressive Farmer* about a manufacturing engineer who became a pig farmer. He put them on concrete in wired pens with no mud and cleaned their droppings with strong hoses and squeegees. The pigs remained clean, and because they walked on the pavement, their hindquarters were stronger and the meat was much—"

"*What* are you prattling on about, Celia?" I ask. "And *why* would you voluntarily read *Progressive Farmer*?"

Patrick snickers next to me, but because I can read his thoughts, I know he's wondering the same thing. Celia Nichols: tall, pretty, smart, rich, and she spends her time reading a farming magazine. I don't get it. But it's what makes Celia, Celia.

She gives me one of her trademark shrugs. "One needs to broaden one's informational horizon and be knowledgeable on a variety of subjects."

I give her the stink face; I don't buy it.

"Okay! I don't know. It was there. I was bored. It happens. Deal with it, K."

I hug her and we laugh together. We move down the line of display cases to a large map of General Sherman's March to the Sea and the path that it took through Radisson. Fortunately, he left the small city in pristine condition.

"Well, pristine if you don't consider all the livestock his men took," Patrick puts in, obviously reading my thoughts.

"Confederate sympathizer?" I ask with a brow raised.

"Hardly. There's nothing right about a person owning another person. I'm just saying that the Union troops took what they wanted when they were in the South."

Becca adds, "We've certainly found that to be true in our ghost-hunting adventures."

"Check that out," Courtney says. She points to a long bayonet with a shiny casing and a jewel on the handle. "That must have belonged to someone rich."

"Or an officer," Patrick says. "They were the ones with the

best uniforms and the top-notch weaponry. Most of the Confederate Army barely had shoes, let alone ammunition."

Courtney bats her eyelashes at him. "*Who* are you?"

"Patrick Lynn," he says firmly. Then he reaches for my waist and slides me against him. "I'm her boyfriend."

Courtney snickers, and my former adversary surfaces for a moment with a snarky remark. "I see you work fast, Kendall. What would Jason Tillson think of this?"

"Jason left Radisson, Courtney. We've both moved on."

I let the uneasiness with Courtney fade. She's obviously still hurt that Jason dumped her and chose to be with someone like me instead of the popular Miss Perfect she thinks she is. At least she's being sociable instead of throwing applesauce at me like she's done in the past.

Celia steps in to break up the tête-à-tête. "Oh, wow, look. That bayonet did belong to an officer. Patrick was right." She leans in to read. "'Colonel Lawrence Hartsell, Waterbury, Connecticut.' He must have left it behind after the Union encampment."

Next to that is an actual Confederate uniform displayed on a mannequin. "I'm going to try my psychometry," I whisper to Celia.

I spread my fingers out over the worn fabric. In my mind I'm projected down a bright tunnel of memories and emotions. "The person who wore this had his leg amputated at the knee. He enjoyed a pipe every evening and played a . . . violin for fun."

Celia makes notes as I speak.

"He was from . . . a farm outside of Augusta. Oldest son. Died of dysentery a year after Lee surrendered."

I sigh hard as I step away from the relic.

"Look, right here," Celia says. "Worn by Major Theodore McClellan from Belvedere, Georgia. That's just north of Augusta. He lost a limb in the battle for Atlanta and he died in 1866, a year after Lee's surrender at Appomattox." She grins at me. "You're good, Kendall."

"You must be the students from Radisson High," a voice calls out.

We all turn in unison to see a rather stout, bald man in an ill-fitting suit and too-short tie mopping his sweaty brow with a handkerchief.

"That would be us," Sean Carmickle says. "Are you the guy who can help answer these questions the teach wants?"

"I certainly can," the man says. "I'm Louis Pfeiffer from the Radisson Historical Society. All of the items you see are authentic pieces that came from real Radisson families and households that were part of the Civil War."

Celia whips out a digital recorder and begins taping everything Mr. Pfeiffer says.

"We have relics that date back even earlier than the Civil War," he states. Pointing to a case, he says, "Like this piece of pottery here. We've tested it and it goes back to 1837, before the war. They would have used it as a plate, or possibly a cup. And over here, there's a Bible from the Wentworth family, who were rumored to be Yankee sympathizers and who fraternized with the Union troops when they were in Radisson."

"I'm just going to take pictures of everything," Farah says. "You know, a digital homework assignment."

"I don't think that'll be enough for Mr. Rorek," I say.

Stephanie raises her hand like she's in elementary school. "I've always wondered if there were any safe houses on the Underground Railroad in Radisson."

Mr. Pfeiffer swabs at his sweaty face again. "There's nothing in any of the historical or city records to indicate that."

My vision clouds for a moment to a scene of a slave family sneaking out an underground tunnel that opens into a field in the dark of night. I blink hard to focus on what I'm seeing, but as quickly as the image appeared, it's gone.

"Are you all right, K?" Celia asks.

"Yeah. Mascara in my eye."

*Why lie, Kendall?* Patrick asks in my head.

*It was just a flashing image.*

*I saw it too.*

*What does it mean?*

*I don't know, but I'm sure we'll find out.*

"Pay attention," I whisper to Patrick.

Mr. Pfeiffer continues to showcase things in the exhibit, and I listen closely and look to my history assignment to make sure I don't miss a thing. However, my fingers begin tingling like I slept with my limbs bent up the wrong way, and now there are millions of ants crawling up and down my arms.

Everyone around me is either halfheartedly paying attention to Mr. Pfeiffer or not taking him seriously at all. Everyone but Celia, who is hanging on his every syllable.

That voice inside my head—which rarely leads me astray—tells me something is not right here. Perhaps that danger Anona spoke of. The other kids are laughing and cutting up and poking fun at the uniforms, the aprons, the shoes people wore back then. Don't they realize what a time of trouble and turmoil the Civil War was? They're literally surrounded by historic buildings and artifacts that are teardrops of our American history. There's nothing funny about brother killing brother, about slaves kept against their will, or about a nation torn in two.

Anger boils and bubbles inside me and I'm sure my face shows something is toying with me, baiting me, and pushing me over the edge. I curl my fingers into a fist in preparation for fight or flight. What is doing this to me? What is making me so annoyed and ill at ease? Something's here. A spirit, perhaps? Of another belligerent soldier? A townsperson who doesn't realize the Civil War is over? A slave looking for that elusive Underground Railroad?

I slip my hand up to my temples and rub, hoping it'll knock the answer loose. Something is undeniably here.

Patrick is on to me and he comforts me with a gentle hug. "Kendall? Are you okay?"

"I most definitely am *not* okay. Don't you feel it, Patrick?"

"For once . . . no."

Becca and Celia seem to sense something is looming as well.

It's there.

Something historic.

Something delicate.

Something important.

Something . . . sinister.

Patrick catches my eye and nods.

Yep, now he's feeling it too.

I strain my vision up ahead, to the next case.

And that's when I see *it*.

Every hair on my body is standing at attention.

## Chapter Four

At first glance, it doesn't appear to be anything threatening.

It's just sitting there in the glass case. The one past the antique field plow and next to the box of useless Confederate money.

"What is that?" Shelby-Nichole asks.

"It's a doll, silly," Stephanie says.

"It's not just any doll," Celia corrects. "That's the one."

"You're quite right, young lady," Mr. Pfeiffer says.

I move toward the glass for a closer look, away from the glare of the overhead spotlight. My eyes shift left and right to take in the sight of the very, very old, ragged dirty doll sitting in a small rocking chair. Although his face is plain fabric and his eyes are made from scratched black buttons, he seems to have life in him. As if this doll is gazing right at you and into you.

"*That* is the creepiest damn thing I've ever seen in my entire life," I manage to say.

"I couldn't agree with you more," Patrick says from behind me.

"It's just a ratty old doll," Farah says. She moves around back to get a better angle on the antique toy.

Stephanie screws up her face. "I'm with Kendall. That thing is over-the-top creeptacular."

Farah lifts her small Nikon camera to grab a shot. Mr. Pfeiffer stops her. "I wouldn't do that if I were you."

"Why not?" she asks.

He hesitates and then swallows hard, judging from the action of his bobbing Adam's apple. "The doll has . . . a story."

Becca crosses her arms across her chest. "Okay, now he's got my attention."

Mine too. Is it this creeptard of a doll that's been sending out the negative energy I'm picking up like a Geiger counter? Waves and waves of hatred, bitterness, and, dare I say, intent to commit malice?

Celia moves forward with her recorder stretched out so as not to miss a word of this story. Everyone else gathers around, listening.

Pointing to the case, Mr. Pfeiffer says, "This is Xander the Doll. He was owned by Robert Townsend Farnsworth in the late eighteen hundreds, following the war. His father was a very prominent member of Radisson society, and Robert was the youngest of sixteen children."

"Sixteen?" Courtney spits out. "That poor mother of his! Her stomach must have had a zipper on it."

"That's how they had babies back then," Farah notes to her cheerleader partner.

"Shhh, I want to hear this," I say firmly. Patrick's hand grips my hip and I know he's picking up the hinky vibe from this doll as well.

"Carbon dating on Xander's clothing shows that he dates back to the eighteen seventies, post Civil War. Legend has it that he came to the Farnsworth family from their slave nanny, Althea. She took care of all sixteen of the Farnsworth children, but she took a special shine to Robert, the youngest." Mr. Pfeiffer walks around the case, carefully inspecting Xander. "You see, Althea was bought by the Farnsworths from a man who traded stock from the West Indies."

I almost growl at the thought of another human being considered stock. But I listen up and don't say anything.

"In the West Indies, in Haiti, Althea was rumored to have practiced the religion of voodoo as a girl and was even thought to be a *manbo,* or priestess, who could invoke the voodoo deities."

Celia speaks up. "Yeah, but isn't *voodoo* just a scary word for mixing African culture with the beliefs of the Roman Catholic Church? I mean, we throw around the word *voodoo* like it's a curse when it's really very religious and based heavily in Catholicism."

Mr. Pfeiffer harrumphs. "I'm not here to teach you theology, son. I can only share the history of this family and their artifacts as I know it."

"So, this Althea chick made a voodoo doll of the kids?" Dragon asks, quite fascinated by the whole theory.

"Not exactly," Mr. Pfeiffer says. "She actually made Xander the Doll and gave him to Robert as protection. From what, our historic documents don't show. All we know is that Althea was accused of making charmed objects that enchanted the children to the point where they were uncontrollable by the parents. Shortly after Reconstruction, Althea tragically was lynched by . . . someone."

"Sorry, but I don't believe all this voodoo crap," Kyle states.

"Language, son," Mr. Pfeiffer snaps.

"Sorry."

Molten heat emits from the glass case, almost like the summer sun radiating off the hot pavement. Invisible waves of energy surround this figurine. I bet if we had an electromagnetic field detector, it would be registering off the charts right now.

"Is this a voodoo doll of the boy Robert?" I ask.

"As I said," Mr. Pfeiffer continues, "it is thought that Althea made him as protection for Robert, but it seemed that over the years, as Robert grew older, all sorts of strange incidents and accidents occurred. Xander the Doll was often blamed for wreaking the havoc and destruction. Nothing could ever prove the doll was animated, yet people swore it was."

"How did Xander the Doll come to be in your possession?" Patrick asks, obviously as fascinated as I am.

"The Farnsworth family's last heir donated the property, including the house and all of its items, to the Radisson Historical Society. In fact, our office is based at Farnsworth House, right on Main Street, but we don't allow visitors anymore. Xander the Doll was in a trunk in the attic and so we moved him to a chair in what was thought to be the room Robert shared with his brothers. People with the historical society would often find Xander the Doll in different locations in the house, never in the chair. About twenty years ago, he was placed in this protective case."

"To keep him from wandering around?" Sean asks with a snicker.

"To keep him preserved," Mr. Pfeiffer corrects.

I'm itching to do some psychometry on this doll. "May I hold him, Mr. Pfeiffer?" I ask politely, hoping that will get me what I want.

"I'm afraid not, dear. No one is allowed to touch Xander. He doesn't like it."

Sean, Jim, and Dragon can't hold in their laughter.

"Dude! It's a frickin' doll!" Dragon exclaims.

"And you need to respect history and folklore, young man," Mr. Pfeiffer states.

Celia steps up to the squat man, towering over him. "Hey, Mr. Pfeiffer, can the ghost huntresses do an investigation at Farnsworth House? That would be totally awesome!"

"I'm afraid not."

"No?"

"No."

"Why not?" I ask before Celia can.

"Because it's private property."

"Your offices are in there," Becca says.

"Our offices are in an addition off to the side of the house. The rest of the property is kept up by a gardener and a house-keeper who are paid through a trust from what's left of the Farnsworth estate. We merely oversee it."

"What's the point of having a historical *society* in a historic building if you don't take advantage of it?" Celia asks, frustration flowing from her.

I know the answer, though, clearly reading each bead of sweat on Mr. Pfeiffer's face. He's not afraid of the house or what historical facts it might render. He's afraid of Xander the Doll. The house is Xander's, and Mr. Pfeiffer doesn't want to do anything to anger the doll.

*If only I could get my hands on Xander.*

*Doesn't look like that's a possibility.*

*Pfeiffer's being stubborn.*

*Pfeiffer's being superstitious.*

*And I'm being curious. I've never felt such a pulsating vibe from an object before.*

*There's definitely something to the folklore of Xander the Doll.*

*Do you think it has a voodoo curse?*

*I wouldn't know.*

*How could I have been in Radisson this long and not known about this legend?*

*He's protected. Hidden away. Besides, no one here picks up things like we do. Let it go, Kendall. Write your history report and forget about Xander.*

*If I can . . .*

Farah raises her camera in front of her, centering Xander the Doll on the display screen. "Oh, I need a picture of this."

Mr. Pfeiffer holds up his hand. "Again, I wouldn't do that if I were you, miss. Xander does *not* like to have his picture taken. People who have snapped his photo in the past have had very bad luck follow them. Some say they're even cursed."

"Listen to him, Farah," I say.

"It may be so," Celia agrees.

Farah scoffs at him, her green eyes blazing with disbelief. "Oh, you're kidding me. I don't believe in any of that stuff." She starts to take a picture again, but Courtney, of all people, stops her.

"What?" Farah asks.

"Don't do it," Courtney says in a ghostly whisper.

"Why not? It's just a picture."

"Don't mess around with this stuff, Farah. Believe me. I know what I'm talking about." Courtney should know. We ghost huntresses had to rid her of a spirit oppression that had taken up residence inside her because she was dabbling with something she knew nothing about. We never told anyone about Courtney's oppression, and to this day, I'm not sure who else knows. But it's good that Miss Popularity and Head Cheerleader is trying to be the voice of reason.

Farah hugs her friend and laughs. "Girlfriend, you're talking crazy. It's just a picture. Besides, I can't turn in my photographic history assignment without this crazy-ass doll."

She lifts her camera again and takes a couple of pictures as she laughs. Sharp daggers of pain punch me behind the eye sockets as I watch the flash hit the glass. Patrick grabs me to hold me up. He winces too at the next flash.

Next thing I know, Sean, Jim, and Dragon jump into Farah's picture. Sean poses all gangsta-like, and Jim gives the Hawaiian hang-loose sign. Dragon waggles his tongue while trying to look all tough. Farah just giggles and continues to snap photo after photo.

There's movement behind the glass.

*Did Xander just move?*

*No, but the bear dropped from his arm.*

"Honestly, y'all," Courtney begs. "Stop it. Seriously. Be cool."

*I swear I saw Xander move. He blinked.*

Patrick snickers. *His eyes are buttons.*

*His eyes are real.*

*He's totally sneering.*

Celia steps between the photo session and the raggedy doll. "Don't you think that's enough?"

Farah and Sean give Celia an army salute and collapse laughing. "Come on, y'all," Farah says. "Let's go ride the Ferris wheel."

Courtney looks back at me with worry in her usually confident eyes. I nod in return. There's not really anything we can do now. Teens will be teens, as they say. She trudges off to join the rest of her clique.

I reach for Patrick's hand and squeeze tightly as I glance over at Xander the Doll. The bear is back in his arm. No idea how that happened. Maybe I didn't really see it drop in the first place. Who knows anymore?

"So, what happens now, Mr. Pfeiffer?" Celia asks.

He lifts his shoulders. "No one ever believes a curse until something happens to him." Then he laughs it off. "It's just a good story, kids. Don't look so somber."

"It's sort of in our makeup to be that way," Celia explains.

Becca, Shelby-Nichole, and I all nod.

"You really won't let us investigate Farnsworth House?" Celia asks, taking one more shot.

"There's no reason to, young lady. I guarantee you it's not haunted."

"Oh, sir," Celia says, "you'd be surprised how little *isn't* haunted in Radisson." She pulls something from her pocket. "Here's my card, in case you change your mind. Or in case things start happening that are attributed to Xander."

Mr. Pfeiffer chuckles hard and holds his large belly in a Santa-like pose. "I'm sure your friends will be fine. Xander the Doll's story is just a myth, nothing more. Something good to roll out for the county fair and help students with a history assignment."

Famous last words.

Patrick and I share a knowing glance.

Something will indeed happen.

## CHAPTER FIVE

I DIDN'T GET MUCH SLEEP LAST NIGHT thanks to the sugar rush from way too much cotton candy and the major ick factor I got from Xander the Doll.

Something just ain't right with the toy.

"Good morning, sunshine," Loreen says to me as I walk into Divining Woman ten minutes before noon on Saturday. "Rough night?"

"You have no idea."

She squints her eyes at me and focuses. "Bad carnival food and an encounter with the paranormal."

I set down my purse, chai tea, and car keys and plop into a chair next to a small table in back. "Now *that* doesn't take a psychic to figure out."

I fill her in on Xander the Doll, how my friends blew off the warning, how concerned I am over what might happen, and how my over-carbohydrated stomach rebelled and kept me awake most of the night.

"And I'm supposed to have this awesome, romantic evening

with Patrick and I'm going to look like the star of *Night of the Living Dead*."

Loreen giggles and comes over to give me a hug from behind. "Don't worry, Kendall. Patrick and Mass were up until all hours of the morning talking philosophy and religion, playing guitar—did you know Mass played?—and making omelets."

I suppress a weak laugh. "Seriously? I mean, I can see everything but the cooking part. Father Mass is a chef?"

A twinkle comes to Loreen's eyes. "The man does know how to make a mean breakfast."

"Loreen! He's a man of the cloth!"

Her mouth drops open. "Kendall Moorehead! I was not insinuating—"

The laughter bubbles out now, bringing me to life like I've had a whole carton of 5-Hours. "Oh, you most certainly *were* insinuating."

She purses her lips and then returns to the front counter. She shouts, "Just do some tarot-card readings, why don't you?"

I'm still chuckling when I hear my phone buzzing and glance down. I don't recognize the number, so I let it go to voice mail. When I check the message, I almost fall out of my chair.

"Umm . . . yes, Miss Ghost Huntress? This is, umm, James Pendergrass. I e-mailed your website about the"—his voice lowers to a whisper, as if he doesn't want someone to hear— "the haunted sandwich in my house." Oh, for heaven's sake!

"The sandwich has now sprouted arms and legs and is walking around my house. The ghost sandwich is—"

I press *9* as hard as I can to delete this message. This guy is insane. I can't handle it right now.

The overhead bell tinkles as the door opens. It's Mayor Shy.

"Hey, Loreen! Hey, Kendall, do you have time for a quick reading?"

"Is everything okay at your house?" My team cleaned out a pretty mean spirit not long ago. I'd hate to hear that paranormal activity has started up again.

She waves me off. "Fine, fine, fine . . . I'm more concerned about my love life right now, if you know what I mean." She winks at me from behind her glasses.

"Sure, I can give you a reading. Have a seat."

"Let me just use your facilities first."

"You know where it is," Loreen says.

My BlackBerry buzzes again and I suspect it's Patrick waking up after his all-nighter with Father Mass to tell me what we're doing this afternoon and tonight. Only it's not a 404 area code; it's coming from 314. My psychic senses inform me quickly that it's a call from St. Louis. With all that's been going on with schoolwork, Patrick in town, Xander the Doll, and everything, I'd almost forgotten about Andi Caminiti.

"Hi, Ms. Caminiti," I say timidly, not quite believing she'd call me on purpose.

There's silence for a moment. "Hi, Kendall."

Another long pause follows, then she finally breaks the quiet. "Look, I've been thinking a lot about your visit. I apologize for being so rude and dismissive to you, it's just that—"

"Oh, no, ma'am," I say, interrupting. "I know that was, like, totally weird, Mom and me just showing up out of the blue like that. We only thought if we told you the purpose of our visit beforehand, you wouldn't agree to see us. We're the ones who are sorry."

I know she's smiling into the phone. "You're quite the polite young lady."

"Well, yeah. I was raised right."

I grip my cell phone harder as she talks. "It's just that I haven't thought of Andy in a while. I mean *really* thought about him and the possibilities of what happened to him. I think in the back of my mind, I've always believed what one psychic told me: he joined the merchant marines and has been sailing around the world for the last seventeen years."

"It would be easier to trust that he's still alive."

She's crying now. "He'll always be alive in my heart. You don't grow up like we did—so close, sharing everything—and just accept that the other person is gone for good."

I think about the people I've lost—my Grandma Ethel and my real mother, Emily. I didn't have nearly enough time with either of them. Grandma Ethel died suddenly, while she was cooking dinner one night. We didn't even get to say goodbye to her. And Emily . . . Emily who'd been with me my whole life, only I couldn't see or feel her until my psychic awakening here in Radisson. Tears burn my corneas as I think about how she faded away from me at the point when we'd *really* found each other. After all, there's no bond stronger than a mother and her child. A bond I would never know with the woman who gave me life. I can understand Andi's connection with her brother.

I swipe my hand under my eyes and sniffle. "I'm sorry for your loss, Ms. Caminiti. I know it has to be hard for you."

She sniffs too, and in my mind's eye, I see her dabbing her nose with a Kleenex. "My entire family gave up hope that Andy was still alive. My father died not knowing what happened to his son, and my mother got so wrapped up in the social scene of St. Louis that she wouldn't even talk to me about the possibilities of what happened to my brother. She's no longer with us either. And then I had to mull over the idea that my brother had fathered a child."

*A child.* Kind of cold when said child is *moi.*

"I understand" is all I can mutter.

Mayor Shy returns from the ladies' room and sees that I'm on my phone. Although I'm slumped in my chair, I hold up my index finger and she moves over to where Loreen stands. Now they're both watching me with great interest. So much for privacy. I don't mind, though. Loreen is family.

Andi's voice crackles over the phone line. "I've been thinking of you and I'm quite struck by the idea that Andy may have had a child . . . with Emily."

I bolt upright from my hunched position. "So you did know about Emily!"

"I hadn't met her, but she was all that Andy talked about. He was crazy about her."

"She was pretty cool," I say. "I mean, as ghosts go."

I'm sure Andi's digesting that. "No one in the family knew her name. No one other than me, that is. So when you tell me about Emily, I have to assume you have some of these psychic abilities you claim to have."

The cell phone pressed against my ear is emitting so much heat that I'm sweating. Or maybe that's just my nerves. "Trust me. This whole psychic thing is totally new to me. I'm still learning to deal with it."

"I'm sure it can't be easy."

"No, ma'am." I pause and then add, "And neither is not knowing who my father is, or was."

A long sigh sounds out. "I've been thinking about it, Kendall, and I'll agree to it."

"To what?"

"To the DNA testing to see if we're related. Andy was my twin, so we're bound to have similar strands in the old double helix, right?"

Smiling into the phone, I say, "I suppose. I'm not that good in science."

Soft amusement sings out to me. "He wasn't either." Then she tacks on, "I do have a bonus, Kendall."

"Yeah?"

I'm visualizing Andi sitting on the couch in her condo in St. Louis. It's a loft with a lot of open space, white furniture, floor-to-ceiling windows, and long, flowing sheer white curtains. She's got a tattered yellow-satin-covered book on her lap. Then the vision breaks as she continues.

"It turns out that when Andy and I were little tykes, we got into a fight that included my snagging a handful of my brother's hair."

"Ouch!"

"His words exactly," Andi says. "The thing is, the hair came out roots and all. Mother put it in a zip-lock bag and taped it in our baby book with the heading 'Andy's first haircut.'"

"Awww, that's so cute," I say, rocking back in my chair.

"It's not only cute but very important, Kendall. There should be enough of Andy's DNA on those hair follicles to test."

My eyes look like the Canadian side of Niagara Falls, gushing with my thankfulness and hopefulness. "I-I-I . . . can't thank you enough f-f-f-for believing me enough to try."

"It'll take weeks, Kendall. But we'll get it done. I'll call Sarah and make the arrangements."

"Thanks, Andi. I'll never forget this."

Another pause. "Let's just take it one step at a time, Kendall."

"You bet."

We say our goodbyes and I collapse onto the tarot-card table in exhausted yet relieved tears; I might be on the right path to finding my paternity. I hear the footsteps of Mayor Shy and Loreen as they pad over to me.

Through a sheen of tears, I gaze up at Loreen and smile. She places a hand on my shoulder and she . . . knows. She's aware of everything that just transpired.

She smiles so sweetly at me. "You've found your family, Kendall."

After the phone call with Andi Caminiti, the weekend flies by in a blur. Patrick and I hang with Celia, Clay, Dragon, and Becca at the bowling alley on Saturday night before returning to my house for a make-out session on the front-porch swing. Well, until Buckley and Eleanor decided to chase after each other and use the swing as an interstate in their fur war.

True to her word, Mom made Yankee pot roast on Sunday and filled Patrick's tummy so full you would have thought it was Thanksgiving at the Mooreheads'. My parents like him, though. I can tell. Must be all his military living and the *sirs* and *ma'ams* that he sprinkles in his conversation. Whatever it is, I'm happy.

Until six thirty comes and Patrick's Kia is packed with his guitar, duffle, and a to-go box from Mom for his forty-five-minute-long trip north to Duluth.

I hurl myself at him, hugging him as tightly as I possibly can. "I wish you lived here."

He kisses the top of my hair. "Me too, Kendall. Me too. At

least I'm closer, you know? Could be worse. I could still be in Tampa."

I bury my face in his chest. "I don't want to think about it."

His finger moves under my chin and he lifts my face to his. We meet in a sweet breath of a kiss that sends a volt of current all the way down my legs. He nibbles on my bottom lip and I sigh as I dissolve into his kiss. So soft. So tender. So sexy. And with our mind connection, I know what he's thinking too.

*So cute.*

*So much fun.*

*So . . . mine.*

"You're mine too," I say when we break for air.

Patrick stretches his arm to push me away. "You. Stay right there or I'll never leave. And I'll flunk out of school and not get into a good college and have to work a minimum-wage job just to pay the bills and it will all be your fault 'cause you didn't let me leave."

I burst into giggles and take two steps backwards.

"See you Friday, cutie." And then he winks.

"It's going to be a long-ass week."

He slips into the car, rolls the window down, and cranks the engine. "I know, but you're tough and you can do it."

I pout. "DNA testing on top of this whole Xander the Doll thing?"

"Neither of which you can control," he says. I hear the gear shift into reverse. "Take care of my girl."

I kiss my fingertips, extend my fingers, and blow at him. He catches the kiss and puts it on his heart. Awww . . . swoooooon!

"Call me when you get home," I shout as he turns around in our gravel driveway.

*You know I will.*

And then his little black car drives out of sight.

I walk back into the house and shut the front door behind me, and Mom steps out of the den, her reading glasses perched on the end of her nose. She beams a smile at me and then walks over to hug me.

"I like this one," she says. "He has his head on right."

"I like this one too."

"And don't you worry about the DNA testing. I've got it set up for Wednesday at my office. It'll be quick and easy and I'll be there with you."

"Thanks, Mom," I say, hugging her back.

"Now scoot upstairs and get your homework done. I'm sure you've put it off all weekend."

I look up at the ceiling, feigning innocence.

"I know you so well, Kendall."

"Love ya; mean it!"

"I know you do, sweetie."

Patrick's right. Mom's right. It'll be okay.

*The breeze blows my hair, loosening the curls I spent an hour with the curling iron to shape.*

*Becca's somewhere nearby spinning a mix of Deadmau5 and*

*Armin van Buuren into a funky House beat that has my foot tapping . . . or maybe that's my heart beating like crazy.*

*Anxiety surrounds me.*

*Unease trips me over my feet.*

*Suddenly, the music stops. Blackness surrounds me. I'm moving through a dark tunnel. Whispered fingers of a spider's web tickle my face in an invisible snare. I swat around left and right to free myself of the entanglement, only to stumble on the stairs leading down, down, down—into what?*

*A growl sounds out. Not exactly demonic in nature. More like in annoyance at being disturbed. A cry. A shout. Piercing blackness with nowhere to go.*

*My hands feel in front of me looking for anything to grab hold of. Nothing.*

*Cold air.*

*A stream of light from an unknown source.*

*A figure near the floor in the shape of a boy.*

*No, not a boy. A doll.*

*It's Xander.*

*He laughs at me. Hard. A cackle that resounds off the clay walls of the deep cave. I cover my ears with my hands, pressing hard, hard, hard, yet I can still hear his shrieking chortle.*

*"You can't stop me," he hisses.*

*Snap.*

*I'm out of the cave and moving with great speed down the hallway at Radisson High. Xander is there. In the hallway. In the lunchroom. In my history class. Then he's standing at the corner of the square,*

*downtown. He's waiting for me when I come down the stairs for break-
fast.*

*"What do you want from me?" I scream to the doll. A doll that is
preserved in a museum case, I remind myself. "What? What do you
freaking want from me?"*

*His button eyes glare at me. Waves of hatred swirl around him.*

*"I'm not the one who did anything! I didn't break the rule or
tempt the curse."*

*Farah's cheesy pictures that are plastered all over her Facebook site
flutter by like turning pages. Jim. Farah. Sean. Dragon. All of them.
Stupid pics and poses with a doll. The hits on the Like button soar
into the thousands.*

*Is everyone crazy? God knows I feel like I am!*

*Anona appears through the mayhem, her eyes conveying concern.*

*"You can do nothing to stop it."*

*"Stop what?" I beg to know.*

*"They brought it on themselves."*

*"Are you telling me this curse is real, Anona?"*

*Xander the Doll is at her feet staring at me with those eyes until
suddenly he blinks and blood pours from his eye sockets and—*

"Ahhhhhhhhhhhhhhhh!"

My scream is more muffled than it sounds in my head.

As I flail about, sheets and blankets fly, as do Natalie, Buckley,
and Eleanor, who are curled up on the bed. Eleanor meows
her displeasure and hops down with a grunt. Buckley readjusts,
and Natalie jumps over to the chair with Sonoma the Bear. My
chest rises and falls with each labored breath and I pray hard

that God will slow my heart down to a reasonable rate and not one in need of medication.

What. The. Hell. Was. That. All. About?

As I struggle to breathe like a normal person, I reach forward and tug my gray and white cat Buckley into my lap. He's sound asleep again, so he doesn't fight me. He just lightly purrs as I hug, pet, and kiss him. There's something calm and soothing about petting a kitty cat that returns blood pressure to normal levels without Lipitor or Crestor or anything else that ends with a -*tor*. Actually, those are for cholesterol, I think, but it doesn't matter right now.

I've had ridonkulous dreams before, but this one was *chilling*. So real, too. The earthy smell of the damp clay tunnel remains in my olfactory system. I scratch at my face even now to rid it of the phantom spider web. And that damn doll with the button eyes. What was *that* all about? No good can come from having any association with a story as mucked up as that of the Farnsworths with their Haitian slave nanny, sixteen children, voodoo protective charms, and God knows what else. I don't know if I'm up for this one.

Then I think of all I learned out in California on my retreat. How the spirit guides and the totem animals spoke directly to me with the message that I have to use my gift to help others. It's my duty in life to find and guide lost souls. I cannot fear. Oliver told me so. Loreen tells me so. Father Mass tells me so. Mom tells me so and even cross-stitched this Bible verse into a throw pillow for me:

*Fear not, for I am with you;*
*be not dismayed, for I am your God;*
*I will strengthen you, I will help you,*
*I will uphold you with my righteous right hand.*

*—Isaiah 41:10*

My eyes lift to the ceiling and I pray with all of my might. "Lord, I'm really gonna need your strength on this one if it's as bad as I think it's going to be. Amen."

# CHAPTER SIX

WEDNESDAY AFTER SCHOOL, I head to Mom's office.

"I can't do this, Kendall," Mom says as she puts down the syringe.

I slouch in the chair at the doctor's office and glance down at my left arm. The blue rubber band is knotted on my upper arm and my hand is balled into a fist. Mom was *this* close to puncturing me with the needle before she chickened out.

She flips off the tight plastic gloves and stacks them on the table in surrender. "I can't hurt my baby like this."

"Mom, please—"

"I can't do it, Kendall."

"Mom, you do this every day to other people's babies," I say, a bit snarkily. I just want this over and done with. Needles are not my friend and I totally gag whenever I watch my own blood drain into those little glass vials. If my mom does it, though, at least I'll know it's being done with love.

"That's different," she says. "Don't you remember? I cried when you got your ears pierced. I can't cause you pain."

I snicker at the memory of my sitting at the Earring Pagoda

in the mall as Mom was over in the corner crying. Bless her little heart.

She reaches over and releases the rubber band meant to help with the blood flow.

"Mom, we have to get this done. Andi Caminiti agreed to the test. *I* can't be the one to back out."

Mom flattens her lips together. "Bernadette, can you come here?"

A tall African American woman dressed in white with fantastic braids past her shoulders comes around the corner. "Yes, Sarah?"

Mom indicates the labwork form on the desk. "This is my daughter Kendall. We need to pull vials of blood to send off for a DNA test."

Bernadette smiles warmly at me. I shift my eyes to my mother and then roll them a bit. Bernadette totally gets it.

"And you can't stick your own baby. I understand. Move aside."

The nurse reties the blue rubber band and instructs me to make a fist. Before I know it, the shiny needle pricks my skin and slides into the vein in the crook of my arm. *Oww, oww, oww.* I pinch my eyes shut when I see the blood begin to fill the vial. I know this has to be done to determine if Andi and I are related, but seeing the worry painted on my mom's face almost breaks my heart.

With my right hand, I reach out to her, and she threads her fingers in mine. I know she and Dad both support me in this effort to get closure on my birth parents. However, I know they fear losing me. I clutch her hand tightly to let her know how much I appreciate her—as well as to fight the pain. Damn, this hurts!

Bernadette pulls the needle out and says, "There you go, sweetheart. Let me just put a Band-Aid on that for you."

She swabs the area with alcohol and then applies the sticky pad to my arm. I'm sure I'll have a whompus-size bruise there later today.

"Sarah, did you get the hair-follicle samples yet?" Bernadette asks while labeling my blood.

"Yes. They're already bagged and tagged."

I rub at the spot at the back of my skull where the hair was plucked.

"Now what?" I ask both my mother and Bernadette.

"All of the samples will get packaged up in a special medical-supply envelope and left for FedEx to pick up and take to the lab in Connecticut," Bernadette explains. "It'll be a few weeks, but don't you worry." She pats my arm and returns to whatever she was doing before Mom called to her.

"So, some scientist with a lab coat and a microscope will determine if my DNA matches up in any way with the Caminiti family."

"That's pretty much it," Mom says with a sigh of relief.

I finger the Band-Aid on my arm, watching a small spot of blood seep through.

Now all I can do is wait.

———

Celia's leaning against my car when I leave the doctor's office. "Everything come out all right?"

"Yep."

She frowns. "Get it? 'Come out all right'? 'Cuz you just had, like, blood drawn?"

"I get it."

"It wasn't funny, was it?" She looks sorely disappointed.

I laugh and pat her on the shoulder. "Sorry, Cel. My mind is in ten thousand other places." The DNA test. My dream. Xander the Doll. My history paper. Everything.

"I'm here to help," she announces. "So what are you doing your Civil War paper on?"

"I haven't the foggiest clue. With so much going on, I haven't even thought of it yet."

She holds up her hands. "Maybe you should write about all of our paranormal adventures and how they relate to Radisson's part in the war."

"That's not exactly historic."

"Just a thought." Standing tall, she says, "We have an appointment with Mr. Louis Pfeiffer to talk to him more about Farnsworth House and Xander the Doll."

My mouth drops open. "How'd you pull that off?"

Celia whistles for a moment and then smiles. "Let's just say that Mega-Mart has recently made a substantial charitable contribution to the preservation of Radisson's precious history."

I smack her on the arm. "You didn't!"

"No, *I* didn't. But my dad did it for me," she says through a bright grin.

"Celia, you rawk!"

She shrugs. "Mega-Mart needed the tax write-off." She opens my car door for me. "Shall we?"

I grin like the Cheshire cat. "You're good."

Ten minutes later, we're parked in the driveway of the old Farnsworth mansion, better known now as the home of the Radisson Historical Society. A very sweaty, nervous-looking Mr. Pfeiffer opens the door and greets us begrudgingly.

"This is highly against our rules," he says flatly, not letting us through the large oak doorway that he's standing in.

Celia crosses her arms over her chest. "Mr. Pfeiffer, I'm sure if you talk to the board and advise them of the substantial amount of money donated by Mega-Mart, they will have no problem with two innocent high school girls coming into the house, taking a look around, and writing a school paper on it."

He steps aside.

Score one for Celia Nichols. Girl's got backbone.

"Is Xander the Doll here?" I ask with a bit of trepidation.

"He is," Mr. Pfeiffer says. "He is in his room upstairs and is strictly off-limits except for special displays."

"He's in his room?" Celia repeats.

"The room he shared with Robert Townsend."

"Is he still in the glass case?" I ask, just to make sure. I really don't need that doll coming to life and stalking me like he did in my dream.

"He is indeed."

Somewhat relieved, I let out a pent-up breath. "Thanks, Mr. Pfeiffer."

"No pictures," he says. "And don't touch anything."

"Yes, sir," I say politely.

"And no—"

"We've got it, we've got it," Celia says.

He scurries off to another part of the house, leaving us standing in the foyer. The place is in pristine condition, with well-polished hardwood floors, expensive Chinese rugs, and detailed oil portraits of the home's former inhabitants. To the left is a formal sitting room; to the right, what looks to be a music room. We walk down the long hallway, which opens up into a huge great room with settees, chairs, sofas, tables, and a lot of marble accents scattered about. A massive fireplace with dark wood trim on the mantel dominates the room.

"You could fit about ten people in that fireplace," Celia exclaims.

"Or at least cook for ten people," I add.

"Oh, they wouldn't have cooked in here. That is for warmth and entertainment. There's probably a hearth in the kitchen just as big."

We wander through the great room and into the back, where there's a bedroom that's been turned into an office. Boxes upon boxes of papers are stacked from floor to ceiling. I recognize many of the family names we've run across in our ghost hunting: Parry and Biddison, to mention a couple. Of course, most of the boxes are labeled *Farnsworth*.

Celia moves to open one of the boxes, but I stop her. "He said no touchy."

"Yeah, but he's sweating like a prostitute in church. You think I'm going to do what he says?"

This time I laugh extra hard. "Okay, *that* was funny."

Before she opens the lid, though, I stretch my hands and wave them over the boxes, looking for something that speaks to me. A humming sound buzzes in the room like many voices whispering at once. Are ghosts of the Farnsworth family trying to tell me something?

I touch the arm of one of the chairs, and at once my ears are filled with shrieking cries of terror and torture. Could this be the resonance of injured or beaten slaves? The tears are more childlike, though, begging *Stop* and *Don't do it*. I remove my hand as if it's been burned and shake off the contact.

"Anything?"

I don't want to say for sure as I can't attribute the cries, so I just say, "The usual stuff."

Celia pulls her EMF detector out of her backpack and begins sweeping the room for readings.

"Don't let him see you using that," I say.

She nearly claps. "I've got a huge spike over in this corner."

"There's nothing here that should really set that off."

"I know. Are you feeling anything?"

I point to three boxes of Farnsworth material. "I'm getting the sense that we should look through those."

"Hmm ... how do we do that if we can't touch?" Celia asks.

I plop down on the floor and cross my legs. "Let me see what I can pick up."

I close my eyes and steady my breathing, letting the energy of the building flow around me. My hands hover above the boxes, palms itching as the information is nearly vacuumed into my skin.

"I'm getting the name Phillip Farnsworth," I say. I breathe deeper and let the house's memories speak to me. My bones rattle as I begin sensing times gone by. Images flash in color and in black-and-white, fluttering through the years so long ago and letting me peek at the Civil War world of the Farnsworths'.

With my eyes still closed, I describe what I see to Celia. "Phillip Farnsworth, the patriarch of the family, was allegedly from noble blood in Great Britain. However, he owed a ton of money to several people back in the early ... umm ... seventeen forties. Wow, that was a long time ago."

"This is all good, Kendall," Celia says. "Keep going."

I fill my lungs with air again and center my thoughts. The images come to me. "Farnsworth was shipped off to the penal colony of Georgia to live in debtors' prison."

Celia giggles like a schoolgirl and I let my hands drop to my lap. "What?"

She laughs again and says, "You said *penal.*"

"Oh, good God, Celia! Get serious."

She tries her best to stop laughing. "I don't know what's gotten into me. Must be the nitrous oxide remnants from the dentist filling my cavity after school."

"You're drugged up? Celia!"

"I'm okay, I'm okay . . . go ahead."

I sigh hard and try to get back my connection with the old house. It takes a few minutes, but soon I'm seeing Phillip Farnsworth again, aboard the large vessel that brought him across the Atlantic Ocean to Georgia. "Okay . . . here we go. Farnsworth moved from Augusta to Radisson when he won this property in a hand of poker. He had a full house. The other guy had two queens." Not that that's important, but it's what I'm picking up. "Farnsworth obtained much of the land on the east side of Radisson and made a buttload of money selling the Georgia pines for timber. From then on, the Farnsworth family had vast wealth that was passed on to Phillip's descendants. Not only that, they used the farmland nearby to grow cotton; to do that they needed to purchase many slaves from the ships that came into port from Africa and the West Indies."

"Thus Althea's arrival here."

I'm not seeing Althea. Maybe she's in these memories though. I don't know yet.

"Phillip's son John commanded the large property." Aching stabs pound over my left eye and I'm starting to pick up a musty stale odor. "Are you getting that?"

"What?" Celia asks.

"That fresh-from-the-boys'-locker-room smell?"

"Thank heavens, no!"

"There's more to this house, Celia, than just bricks and mortar. Something is rotting here. Something that needs to be cleansed—set free."

"As you see," she says. "The historical society only uses a few rooms here. Everything else is pretty much in the condition they got the house in."

"I'm sensing more secrets here than anyone could possibly understand." I drop my hands to my lap in frustration as my psychic headache intensifies. The images are becoming more transparent and it's harder to grasp them. "I wish Patrick were here. We could combine our energies and really see past the dirty panes of history."

Celia bounces in place. "Then y'all could do that mind-meld thing you were telling me about."

"Something like that," I say with a smile.

We walk back out to the great room, where I pick up the scent of roaring fires long gone. This room was once filled with partygoers, food, festivities, music, and many slaves to wait on the wealthy. It now houses books and periodicals from another time, paintings of former residents of the house, and antique furniture that would probably fetch a pretty penny at the Saturday flea market in downtown Radisson.

I glance up at the ceiling. "Celia, something deep inside tells me that the Farnsworths harbored a dark secret. Way darker than we could ever imagine. Darker than the people of

Radisson at the time could realize. There's something that's blocking my ability to see any deeper though. I definitely need Patrick for this. Can you get the team in here for one of our in-depth, full-fledged wired-for-sound ghost hunts?"

Celia places her thumb and forefinger on her chin and rubs. "I'll have to talk to Pfeiffer again. Couch it in terms of investigating the building, you know, for school."

I wait patiently while she goes to find him. The whispers of voices from the past circle me but refuse to speak clearly. They know who and what I am. Something's keeping them at arm's length, though.

"It's okay . . . I'm here to help," I say out loud.

Silence. Only the chirping of the robins outside in the trees.

Celia comes padding back into the room, out of breath. "Okay, he's not happy, but he said he'll talk to the board and get permission. He said he'll remind them of Mega-Mart's recent donation when they make their decision. I can confidentially say that we're in."

I glance about one more time. No more whispers. But the lost souls are there. And I'll help them.

*I'll be back*, I say to the spirits.

"Yep . . . something is *definitely* up here."

## Chapter Seven

Patrick flings himself back on the couch in my den Saturday morning and runs his hands through his thick hair. "Kendall, you can't suspect *everything* of being paranormal."

"But it surrounds me. Everywhere I go. Everything I do. I can't get away from it."

He pats the cushion. "Just relax and enjoy the rest of the weekend with me. Just ignore it the best you can."

I grab my phone from my purse and dial. "Oh, yeah? Well, listen to this."

"You have one new message. Message received at two forty-four P.M. 'Umm, yes, Miss Ghost Huntress, this is James Pendergrass calling again. I'm the one with the haunted sandwich. I really need to know what to do. The sandwich walked out of the house yesterday and into the garage, where it stole my car. I reported it to the police, but they laughed at me. My number is—'" I stop the message.

"Are you kidding me?" I ask, the BlackBerry flat in my palm. "Of course the police laughed at him."

"The guy is obviously insane," Patrick says. "That's not paranormal; that's *ab*normal."

"Well, yeah . . . but what if he's not abnormal? What if he's for real? What if his ham sandwich truly *is* haunted?"

"Did he say it was a ham sandwich?" he asks. "Not turkey or bologna?"

"I think so. I don't remember if he specified whether—"

He continues. "Because I would need to know if there was cheese involved and what condiments might have set off the spirit world. You know, are they against spicy mustard but not yellow mustard, or do they prefer Monterey jack to, say, Swiss?"

I smack him hard on his muscled biceps as he laughs like a hyena. "Who cares what kind of frickin' sandwich it was? This loony tune is calling me on a regular basis, I'm having nightmares about that megacreepy doll, and that *house* down the street was talking to me. A house, Patrick."

He tugs me over to the couch, where he cuddles me next to him. "It's in our makeup to question things we're sensing. I understand. I just don't want all of our weekends together to be spent doing nothing but paranormal things, you know?"

"We went out for pizza last night," I say.

He rolls his brown eyes. "With your ghost-huntress friends."

"And we went back to Father Mass's and watched a movie."

Patrick frowns at me. "Yeah, you Redboxed *Paranormal Activity*."

I'm starting to see a pattern here, one I also fell into with

Jason and that he didn't appreciate either. Maybe I should listen this time. Patrick is right. I rest my head on his shoulder, and his fingers find their way into my hair, stroking through the long strands. I love when he plays with my hair because it makes me feel treasured. My hand runs over his T-shirted chest; he's wearing a brown one with funky guitar designs all over it. I move my finger around the outline of the one closest to me. "I'm sorry. I don't mean to be a boring date."

He sits up. "You're not at all, Kendall. I love being with you. And I know we're both psychic, and dealing with spirits and other entities is just part of our lives. I don't have a problem with it. I just think we both need a break. Like, you know, our parents work during the week and relax on the weekends. Maybe we should look at our paranormal activity in the same way."

"The weekend is the only time I have to spend on my ghost hunting." He frowns a bit. So I add, "And with you."

His face twitches into a half smile. I can tell he's got an idea. "We need to do something unique, fun, and not at all related to ghosts, the paranormal, or anything like that."

"What do you have in mind, Mr. Lynn?"

Patrick leans into me, moves my hair off my neck, and gives me a little nibble behind my ear. Chill bumps break out on both of my arms and I feel like I'm going to burst into a thousand pieces and float up to join the stars in their twinkling activities.

Muffled in my hair he says, "I was thinking . . ." His lips move to my earlobe.

"Yes?"

". . . of doing something outrageously fun."

I tense up a little bit, thinking he might be talking about doing *that*. I'm totally in deep with this guy, but I don't think I'm ready to take *that* step yet. Certainly Patrick wouldn't expect me to do that here at my house. Or worse, at Father Mass's rectory. Right! Like that's going to happen.

Patrick bolts up and his chocolate eyes darken. "Kendall Moorehead! You nasty little thing, you."

"What?"

"I wasn't suggesting we hook up."

OMG! I totally forgot for a sec that he can hear my thoughts when we're this close.

Fire engulfs my face as I am mondo-embarrassed.

He hugs me back to him and laughs. "You're adorable when you get all red like that."

"Stop!" I say, ashamed of myself. I want the earth to swallow me whole. He tickles me, though, and I giggle something fierce. "Patrick!"

Patrick stops, sits up, and pushes his shaggy hair out of his face. "The outrageous thing I had in mind was to take you away from Radisson for a day at the beach."

"The beach?"

"You heard right."

I know I'm looking at him like he's insane in the membrane. "Dude, we live in the middle of the state. The beach is like five hours away." I motion outside through the curtain. "Besides, it's April and it's in the fifties and raining big old chunky droplets that are pounding like tribal drums on Mom's elephant ears on the side of the house."

"O she of little faith," he says as he gets us both up off the couch. "Go upstairs and find your swimsuit. And trust me."

He stoops low and lays a warm kiss on my waiting lips.

A dazzling smile and a twinkle in those Hershey Eyes of his and I'm a goner.

"Okay, whatever you say . . ."

"All right. This is *the* coolest place ever," I say with a huge grin.

Patrick plops a kiss on my shoulder. "Told you to trust me."

"I will from now on. Promise."

Because he and his dad live in Gwinnett County, we can use the indoor water park and aquatic center here in Bethesda Park as residents. Even on a rainy day like today, where the droplets on the top of the car sound like applause, we can enjoy the fun of splashing around in the water like it's spring break again. It's like a beach and a water park all rolled together.

This place is insane! According to the information at the check-in counter, it's over thirty thousand square feet of indoor water fun with a gigamonic leisure pool, a hundred-foot slide that exits and then reenters the building, a river channel, tumble buckets, a vortex, and ceiling spray. I am all over this place. Let me in—woot!

"I lurve it! How did you find this?"

"A guy at school told me about it. He's on the swim team and uses the lap pool a lot for practice. I've come a few times to get my sea legs back."

Patrick had a near-death experience in Barbados way before I met him; it resulted in his blooming psychic awareness when he came to. Because of his being all freaked out about things, he decided to stay out of the water. That is, until he saved my life when I was bodyboarding in California and got dunked all the way to the bottom of the ocean.

I take his face in my hand and turn him toward me. "I'm so happy you're getting back in the water. Do you think you'll start doing SCUBA again?"

"Don't rush me," he says.

"You'll know when the time is right."

"I'm trying, Kendall." He pays the modest fee at the counter for a resident (plus guest) and then walks me over to the glass wall so I can look in. "It's mostly for families with little kids, but hey, we're still kids, right?"

"Damn skippy!"

I wrap my arms around his waist and bear-hug him. "You're the best, Patrick."

He moves back and smacks me with the corner of his beach towel. "Let's get going, missy."

I'm so happy right now I can't even describe it. I'm not thinking about any of that you-know-what stuff. I'm focusing only on having an awesome-filled time with my new boyfriend, Patrick.

He gives a squeeze to my hand as we part ways to head into our respective locker rooms. Once inside, I stash my purse, clothes, and shoes in a secure locker. I check my tankini—not bad—in the mirror before stepping out into the main area. I'm not even going to worry about my hair, just put it up in a messy bun.

A wolf whistle cuts through the air as I emerge from the ladies' and into the warm pool area in my black-and-white flowered top and black bottoms. I put my cell phone underneath Patrick's towel on the bench and do a fake curtsy before trotting over to where Patrick is standing. He's all tan and muscly in his baggy blue Hawaiian-print trunks. His tattoo, Boo, is prominent on his left shoulder, and I slide up to him, pressing my left shoulder against his so our matching tats can "kiss."

"You're so silly," he says. "That's what I love the most about you."

I freeze in my tracks. Wh-wh-what? Did Patrick Lynn just say he loves me? Oh. My. God. I can't believe it. So soon? Is it too soon? Or not? What do I do? What do I say?

*Say you love me too.*

Damn these shared thoughts. Or maybe not. With us, there's no games. No BS. There's none of that typical what-does-he-think-about-me garbage most normal teens go through. I don't need my best friend to question his best friend to get me answers on how he feels about me. He knows. I know. *We* know.

*I love you too.*

Somehow it's easier because we're saying it in our heads and not actually out loud. The time will come for the real words.

He grabs my hand and pulls me toward the beach entry area. "Come on. Let's play!"

At first the water is chilly on my bare feet, then it feels just right, like it's been heated to the perfect temperature. To our left is a water jungle gym with ropes and slides, steps, ladders, and waterspouts.

"I think this was designed for toddlers," Patrick says, tugging me up the stairs with him.

Giggling, I say, "We were once toddlers." Then I dodge the spray of water from the nearby cannon and slip into the spiral slide, which seconds later lands me in the shallow water below.

"Come on, Kendall!"

I shove my soaked hair out of my face and crawl behind Patrick, who's ducked under the water and is heading to the towering poles with buckets on them.

When he surfaces, he pulls himself up on the ledge under the buckets.

"What's going to happen?" I ask. Then I immediately figure it out. Water pours into the buckets and then—*kerrrrrrsplash*—down on us. "Oh my God!" Hence the name *tumble buckets.*

Durr! I scream as Patrick cackles. Both of us are totally soaked and I know I look like a drowned alley cat.

"You look adorable," he says, sweeping his arm around my waist and tugging me into his chest.

"We could probably go a whole day without ever saying an actual word to each other, you know?" I say over my shoulder.

"What fun would that be?" Then he kisses me on my cheek and snuggles a little in the water before—*kerrrrrrrrrsplash*—we get zonked on the heads a second time.

Not wanting to get beat down again, I swim under the water next to Patrick. He's so strong and swift cutting through the pool. I'm so glad he's gotten over his fear and is doing what he loves best. Right before we surface, he reaches over for my hand and smiles at me. A goofy, bubble-filled grin.

We come up inside a circle of water falling from the ceiling.

"Simulated rainforest?" I ask.

"Something like that."

Like we're eleven years old again, we spin around in the small circle inside the simulated rain, splashing each other like there's no tomorrow. A yelp leaves my throat before I even realize how kiddish I'm acting. But it feels amazing. The tingling in my limbs isn't from anything psychic or paranormal. There's no spirit talking to me that I know of, and even if there were, this is *my* time. I'm enjoying life with my boyfriend. At a freakin' indoor water park. Whoever invented this place is totally my new best friend.

Patrick flips to his back and begins stroking away from me. "You have to check this out. Follow me."

I happily do as I'm told, kicking my feet hard in the water and almost knocking a pink noodle out of a little kid's hand. "Sorry!" I call out, although he still gives me a dirty look.

We swim toward the river channel that curves around and around. Patrick takes my arms and pulls me up onto his broad shoulders, almost as though I'm riding piggyback in the water. Strong jets under the stream keep the current swirling in a river formation, so we just—literally—go with the flow.

"Are you having fun?" Patrick asks as we float along.

"Ummm, yeah. Duh!"

"I had to ask," he says.

A sheet of water falls near us from nearby pipes, but Patrick steers us away and around the next bend. I cling to his neck and hold on, not even having to kick or anything for movement. I'm so amazingly relaxed right now that it's not even funny.

"You were right. I needed something like this."

I see his dark head nodding in the affirmative.

We circle back to the mouth of the river, and Patrick points to the left. "Head to the vortex."

Now from what I've learned in science class, a vortex isn't something one necessarily wants to head into. But I follow my boyfriend with great trust.

"Wheeeeee!"

We're zipped into a swirling whirlpool circling clockwise (or counterclockwise, depending on which way you look at it) and just go around and around and around. Patrick hoists me up a little farther on his back and we swing around together through the crystal blue water. I hold his neck and shout like a little girl who has her favorite ice cream sundae presented to her. Everyone here is laughing. Shouting, screaming, playing, and enjoying the thrill of being in the pool on such an icky spring day.

"This was the best idea evah," I say with a laugh as we keep going in circles.

"You're not getting dizzy?" he asks.

"Nope. I could stay in the vortex all day."

Patrick reaches forward for two abandoned swim noodles. "Here, try these." He has me lie on my back, and then he bends the pink one under my armpits and the blue one under my knees. "*Voilà!* Instant floating chair."

I beam at him. "You're a genius."

I haven't been on many dates other than with Jason, but this is the most incredible one of all. Fate totally brought Patrick and me together. We're the same. We understand each other. We're meant to be.

I can't believe it . . . I'm in love again.

And I'm not letting *this* one get away.

# CHAPTER EIGHT

WE SPIN A BIT MORE IN THE CURRENT, and I glance up and see a line forming at the base of a red staircase that leads up to the ceiling. "Is that the water slide?" I ask, craning my neck to get a good look.

"Yeah, it is. You'll love it," he tells me. "It exits outside and then reenters the building."

I shove the noodles aside and stand up. "We've *got* to do that. Like right now," I state, my eyes so wide, I know I must appear as eager as a kid on Christmas morning.

He kisses me soundly on the lips and smiles from ear to ear. "You seriously *are* the cutest thing ever."

I grab his hand and pull him along with me toward the slide. "Come on, you cutie, yourself."

Can't believe I just said that out loud, but he can hear it in my head anyway, so what's the point of playing coy?

Impatiently, I tap my foot as I wait in line behind about six little kids. At least two of them don't meet the height requirements for this ride, but no one seems to care at all. We linger until we see the person spew out of the bottom of the tunnel and into the wading pool to the right of the staircase.

Patrick points up and then to the side. "You jump in up there and it slides you through this tunnel maze outside and then you end up there."

I clap my hands. "I can't wait!"

This is awesome. I'm not stressing about anything at all. Not Mr. Haunted Sandwich or Xander the Doll or anything else that might be trying to speak to me. Today, I'm just a normal teenager on a date with her boyfriend. End of story.

Patrick moves forward a step. "I'm next!"

"Why can't I be first?" I say with a pretend pout.

"Because I want to see you when you get to the end."

"Awww, that's sweet."

"Not really," he says. "I want to see your expression."

I elbow him and laugh. This boy knows how to make me happy.

When a roly-poly eight-year-old slides into the waiting pool, Patrick flashes me a grin. "I'm up! See you at the end, schweetheart."

With that, he bounds up the spiral staircase and out of view. But not entirely out of my vision. I close my eyes and concentrate, seeing that Patrick is sharing his ride experience with me.

*Here we go,* he says to me.

And away!

The tube is filled with about six inches of water and I'm riding down the tunnel with Patrick, seeing what he sees. He takes a right curve first, then a sharp left. Light from the dingy day outside brightens the tunnel in the third turn where the water churns up like a small tidal wave. Left, right, straight, and then—*swooooooooosh*—into the tidal pool.

I open my eyes to see my boyfriend flat on his back in the shallow water, shaking off the ride. Pounding up the staircase, I call down to him, "Now you can ride with me."

He gives me the okay signal and I continue up.

At the top, a bored teenage girl—probably my age—sits on a stool, picking at the split ends of her hair. She must be hard-core loco if she doesn't enjoy this job.

I smile and say hey to her, but all I get is a grunt in return. Whatever. I'm celebrating life today! Patrick has given me a gift and I'm going to take the pleasure of the day to the bank, annoyed fellow teenager aside.

There's a flat landing with a wide mouth that opens into the slide tunnel. I crawl in and position myself forward, feet first, like the instructional poster indicates. God forbid Ms. Split Ends does anything to earn her paycheck other than sit there and look bored to tears.

*Okay, here I go.*

*I'm with you, Kendall.*

Releasing my hands overhead, I push off and I'm into the rushing water, corkscrewing down the slide. The cool water tickles my skin as I slip through the channel. A giggle bubbles up out of my chest and I wave my hands in front of me.

Then everything changes.

The fun stops.

Darkness encompasses me and I blink hard to regain my sight.

Things were going so well.

Until my psychic vision kicked in, blinding me to my surroundings.

*Oh no! Patrick, help!*

This one's a doozy.

While my body continues to zip through the water, my brain is struck with horrifying, vivid imagery. Flashes of metal scraping the pavement. Torn clothing. Screams of pure, out-and-out pain. Blood pooling in a jean-covered wound. A siren in the distance. Rotating blue and red lights. Not of the party kind; the police and ambulance sort.

Someone's hurt.

Bad.

Anona appears to me. Her eyes attempt to be soothing, calm, and gentle. Her words are anything but. "It is happening," she utters.

Anxiousness washes over me, mixing with the chlorine. "What's happening?" I beg.

Anona fades away. Damn these spirit guides and their ambiguousness. Can't they just come out and tell me what's what? And why tell me if I can't stop it?

My vision clears as quickly as it dimmed, and I'm belched

out the bottom of the slide into the shallow pool where Patrick awaits, his brow furrowed with worry.

I gulp in a mouthful of water and immediately begin choking, coughing, and sputtering.

"Kendall!" Patrick wades out to me and gently pulls me to my feet while he pats me on the back.

Air seems in short supply as I try to get a good breath. My chest aches and both my kneecaps feel torn, bloodied, and battered. God, there are times when I *really* hate this empathic thing I've got going.

"Are you okay?" Patrick asks. He hugs me close to him.

I nod, but I don't really mean it. Hot tears mix with the cool water on my skin. Patrick's touch is comforting until his hand stills.

"I saw it too. At least, most of it."

"Who was it, though?"

"It's your friend Dragon," Patrick says flatly. "He's the one."

We step out of the pool and I rush over to where I left my towel, making sure I don't run and get the lifeguard whistle blown at me. The terry cloth feels good on my face as I dab my eyes, which are wet from both fun and sadness.

"What can we do?" Patrick asks. "Was it a premonition or has it already happened? Is there anything we can do to prevent it?"

Frustration overtakes me and I snap, "I don't know! These visions don't come with instructions!"

But my BlackBerry may have the answer. I tug it out from underneath Patrick's towel where I stashed it earlier, and I have three voice mails. Without even checking the messages, I dial Becca ASAP.

"Kendall?" she asks, obviously through tears.

"Becca, what happened to Dragon?"

"How did you—"

"I just know. Tell me."

"He was going home from my house and took the curve too sharply at Jackson Hill. Kendall, he totally wrecked his motorcycle and he's in the emergency room. I'm so scared!"

"We'll be right there."

"It was Xander the Doll," I say to Becca and Patrick when we get to the Radisson hospital an hour later. We meet her outside the ER.

Becca rolls her overly black-lined eyes. "A doll didn't cause Dragon to crash."

"You don't know that."

"Umm, Kendall, I totally believe in ghosts," she says, "based on our investigations and evidence we've gathered. But there's no way in hell that I'm going to believe a Civil War–era toy-slash-voodoo-doll did this to my boyfriend."

Patrick reaches out for Becca's arm. "The most important thing here is that Dragon's okay."

Becca wipes a tear out from under her eye. "I guess so, if

you consider two bloody knees, a separated shoulder, and a busted upper lip okay."

"He's alive," I chime in. "Thank God he was wearing a helmet."

"Well, duh," she replies. "Sorry, I don't mean to be snippy. I'm not good at handling blood and ick and stuff like that. Certainly not from my boyfriend."

"Did anyone see what happened?" Patrick asks.

"My dad did," Becca says. "Dragon had just left my house and Dad was coming back from the grocery store. He told me it looked like Brent swerved to avoid something in the road and then lost control, slid his rice rocket across the pavement."

Patrick and I both wince, and the pain in my knees returns, obviously picking up on what Dragon experienced.

*It was Xander the Doll.*

*You can't be sure.*

*If we can dig into Dragon's memory, we can find out.*

*I'm game if you are,* he tells me in my head.

"Can we see him, Becca?" I ask.

She nods. "Only two can go in at a time, so I'll wait out here."

We walk through the automatic double doors leading to the emergency area. Only a few months ago I made this same journey to see Jason and Taylor after their mom attempted suicide. I felt completely helpless then, but today I'm on a mission to get to the bottom of this.

"We're here to see Brent Dragisich," Patrick informs the nurse at the desk.

"Oh, the boy who had the motorcycle wreck," she says. "He's in room four. He's a bit groggy because of the pain medication, but you're welcome to go back. Only stay a little while. He needs rest."

"Yes, ma'am," I say and then follow Patrick to Dragon's room.

With a sweep of my arm, I move the draped curtain aside and gasp when I see my friend. Both legs are bandaged up, he has an IV running into his hand, and there's a heart monitor and a blood pressure monitor on him for good measure. He's got a nasty bruise on his face, and his left arm is in a sling.

His heavy eyelids part slightly, and he seems to know who we are.

"Dragon, hey . . . it's Kendall and Patrick."

He sleepily grunts an acknowledgment.

"Dude, what happened?" Patrick asks with a light laugh.

Brent's eyes open and close, and he groans while adjusting in the bed. He licks his mouth, and I can see that his upper lip is a cracked mess. Damn! Poor kid!

"Can you tell us what happened?" I press.

His lips move slightly, but the words he's mumbling are hard to understand. Then I hear him say something about "seeing it" and it being "in front" of him.

I elbow Patrick. "Did you hear that?"

"I think I did. Come on, Dragon. Talk to us."

"Sleeeeeeeeepy, man. Gotta . . . sleep."

His head lolls to the side, and I know the medication has gotten to him.

My eyes meet Patrick's and we connect telepathically, each of us having the same idea. He takes Brent's right hand and I take the left. The sterile hospital room fades away, and Patrick's and my joined psychic vision explodes in a colorful burst of patterns and sounds. Much like when I was in Patrick's mind zooming through the water-tunnel slide, I am now in Brent's memories. Patrick is with me and we see everything from Brent's vantage point. He's having a great ride through the streets of Radisson and speeds up a bit too much as he approaches Jackson Hill, which curves around the old cotton mill and has a bit of a blind spot.

It's like we're riding along with him. We see something up ahead that appears to be a small human. A little child, perhaps, standing right in the middle of the road. Brent squeezes the brakes, which lock into place. The front of the bike swerves as he avoids the child, and he overcompensates as he tries to right the bike. The motorcycle wobbles, falls, and then skids across the pavement, bringing Brent along for a not-so-fun ride. I feel his pain again, from the jags in his knees to the excruciating pain in his mouth as he cuts his lip. A small laugh comes from behind the wrecked bike. The laugh of someone in control of this situation. Who purposely tripped up Brent and caused this.

I spin in the vision and come eyeball to buttons with the perpetrator.

The image bursts apart and I lose my grip on Dragon's hand, nearly falling to the floor.

My eyes shift to Patrick, across the bed. "You saw him, didn't you?"

He can't help but nod in agreement.

"You were right, Kendall."

# CHAPTER NINE

LOREEN AND FATHER MASS LAUGH OFF our theory when we're eating Sunday brunch with them after church at the Café Buffet.

Father Mass, my Episcopal priest and Loreen's boyfriend, wipes his mouth with the cloth napkin. "It's just folklore," he says. "It's nothing but a story to tell people so they'll buy a T-shirt or magnet at one of the gift shops in town."

"That's just it," I explain, "Mr. Pfeiffer at the historical society is all hush-hush about the building. They have an office in the back where people can file inquiries and stuff, but you're not allowed into Farnsworth House. Doesn't that defeat the purpose of sharing history? And they've got Xander the Doll stashed upstairs in his own room. Don't you think that's freaky weird?"

Loreen sets her iced tea down on the table. "I have to agree with Massimo, you two. I've seen a lot as a psychic/medium, but I've never heard of a historical doll encased in a glass box in a building moving itself and causing a motorcycle accident to injure someone who'd posed in a picture with it."

"It happened though!"

The older couple at the table next to us glance up from their fried chicken when I raise my voice.

"I'm just saying . . ."

Patrick comes to my defense. "We did a lot of research on the Internet last night and we found out that there's a history of odd things occurring in conjunction with Xander the Doll."

I can tell Father Mass is intrigued. "Such as?" he asks.

Sitting forward, I say, "Robert Townsend Farnsworth was accused of setting fires when he was a little boy, but he attributed the fires to Xander. To sort of punish Robert, his parents made a room in the attic for Xander. He was locked away when Robert was at school or out playing. However, they would always find the door open and the room empty, even when Robert wasn't home."

"That's weird," Loreen says.

"I'm telling you, this doll has powers given to him by that voodoo-priestess nanny."

Father Mass lays his napkin down and pushes his plate forward. "I know you're not one to make stuff up, Kendall, but this one is really out there."

"I know. I couldn't *make* this stuff up. And now I think my friends are cursed because they had their picture taken with the doll."

Loreen creases her brow. "What's that all about again?"

Patrick picks at his half-eaten macaroni and cheese. "Mr. Pfeiffer told us at the fair that Xander didn't like having his picture taken. If you took a picture, bad things would happen."

"Like Dragon's motorcycle accident."

Father Mass folds his hands together. "If it will make you feel better, I'll go over to the hospital this afternoon to see Brent and pray to have any curse removed. Is that good?"

"I would totally appreciate that."

The waitress comes up at that moment with a pitcher in her hand. "Y'all want some more iced tea?"

"I think we're good," Patrick says. I can read the concern in his eyes.

"I'll take the check when you get a chance," Father Mass says.

The waitress smiles through her heavy pink lipstick. "Y'all can't leave without trying the banana pudding."

I sigh. "Thanks, but I'm not exactly in a pudding mood today."

"Just the check," Loreen says with a smile.

Father Mass stands, kisses Loreen on the forehead, and says, "I'm going to the men's room. I'll be right back."

Patrick stands. "I'll go with you."

Loreen and I both laugh, breaking the tension caused by Xander.

"Hey," I call out as they go. "Only girls are supposed to go to the bathroom together."

The waitress sets the check face-down on the table and slides a small to-go box in front of Loreen and me. "Y'all take some pudding home. Whatever's bothering you, it'll make you feel better. Come back to see us!"

Loreen pushes the box at me.

"Thanks." I fiddle with the edge of the Styrofoam, contemplating everything. "I just have this horrible feeling, Loreen, that something else is going to happen. That we're not done with Xander the Doll's destruction."

"Have you tried dowsing and asking questions?"

"That's a great idea." I reach into my purse and withdraw the new jasper pendulum that I got at Loreen's store. It's blue lapis and spins like crazy for me.

I take the stone in my right hand and hold my arm close to my body. "May I ask some questions right now?"

The pendulum swings in a clockwise manner, indicating *yes*.

"Is Xander the Doll, who lives in the old Farnsworth House, real?"

Another clockwise spin.

"That's a bit ambiguous, hon," Loreen says. "Obviously he's real. You've seen him with your own eyes. Watch how you phrase your question."

"You're right." I concentrate and try to think clearly. "Is Xander the Doll causing trouble?"

The pendulum spins *yes* like no tomorrow.

"Did Xander the Doll have something to do with my friend Brent's accident?"

Again, the pendulum gives me a positive response.

Loreen interjects. "Test it to make sure it's not a yes-man pendulum today."

"Do I live in Toledo, Ohio?" I ask. It's the best I could come up with.

The pendulum slows its spin and then begins to rock back and forth horizontally, which indicates my personal *no*.

"Okay then. Will Xander the Doll hurt someone else?"

Not only does the stone turn in the *yes* direction; I also hear something in my head. An echo, as if someone's in a tunnel. An echo that reverberates in my ears. Laughter with a sinister tone to it.

Suddenly, the pendulum is pulled from my hand and tossed onto the top of the box of banana pudding.

"What just happened?" Patrick asks when he and Father Mass return from the men's room.

"My pendulum says Xander will hurt again."

He takes my hand, and the lightning flash of information blinds us both. How does one describe major chaos, confusion, and destruction? How do we pinpoint when these horrible things are going to happen? Who do we warn? Who do we call?

Our hands break apart and Patrick stares at me. "I don't know who's next."

My heart sinks to my stomach and the rumble of just-eaten fried chicken makes me feel like I'm going to be sick. "I don't either."

*Anona . . . give me a sign. Help me. Help me help whoever's in trouble. Help me stop this damn doll and his vengeance.*

But nothing. Anona's not speaking to me.

I stare at Loreen, hoping she might be able to offer guidance. Instead, she pushes her brunch plate away from her, knocking a piece of a fried green vegetable over the side. I stare at the small morsel, watching as she picks it up and returns it to her plate.

"I shouldn't have gotten those. Never been much of a fan," she says.

"I don't blame you. Okra really is an acquired taste that . . ." I trail off as it hits me. "That's it! Okra!"

"What?" Patrick asks.

"Sean Carmickle. His nickname is Okra. He's next, Patrick! We've got to warn him."

Without another word, Patrick grabs my car keys and heads for the door.

Loreen shouts, "Go!"

I just hope we're in time.

I drive my Honda Fit away from the restaurant like I'm hellbent for election—something Mr. Rorek said that I picked up—not even stopping to thank Father Mass for the lunch.

"Go, go, go," Patrick says as the light turns from green to yellow.

"That's the second one I've run!"

"Who cares?"

My hope is that the Radisson police aren't out to make an example of me today. Probably not, since it's not the end of the month and they don't need to make their ticket quota yet. I downshift into third gear and punch through the next light as it's turning yellow as well.

"That's three!" I say, more flustered than ever.

"Don't you have Sean's cell phone?" Patrick asks.

"We're friends, but we're not like close or anything, not enough to swap digits."

*God, please don't let anything happen to him.*

As I approach my house on Main Street, I see Celia standing on the sidewalk waving her long, gangly arms at me to stop. I don't really have time, but girlfriend literally runs out into the street in front of me.

"Hold on!"

I slam on my brakes, throwing Patrick forward a bit until his seat belt pulls him back.

"Are you crazy, Celia?" I scream through the open window.

"Unlock the door."

I press the automatic lock button and she jerks the back passenger door open. "What's going on?" I ask.

Before she can answer, two Radisson police cars come roaring by me with their lights flashing and sirens blaring. I jam the car into first and move out of the way just in the nick of time. The ladder truck and fire engine are fast on the heels of the police, an ambulance in close pursuit behind them.

My psychic headache begins to pound in the middle of my forehead. I glance at Patrick. "Oh no—are we too late?"

"Too late for what?"

"We're trying to stop something before it happens." Then I

go into mother-hen mode. "Nichols, what on God's green earth were you doing running out in front of me like that?"

She leans between the front seats. "That's what I'm trying to tell you. Shelby-Nichole was at the fire station with Mayor Shy doing some sort of Sunday potluck-lunch thing for publicity when the call came in."

I snap my fingers. "Point. Make it. Quickly."

Celia's not offended. She knows me by now. "One thirty-four Sycamore Lane."

Patrick's eyebrow lifts, as if to ask me whose address that is. "I don't know who lives there."

Eyes bulging, Celia shouts, "It's Sean Carmickle's house!"

I floor the gas pedal.

# CHAPTER TEN

I SMELL THE FIRE before I see it.

Acrid gray smoke billows up over the crape myrtles lining Sycamore Lane. Ironic . . . why didn't they name it Crape Myrtle Lane?

Patrick fusses. *Does that really matter now, Kendall?*

I shake out of my funk and park the car a block down the street from Sean's where all of the emergency vehicles have gathered. The three of us climb out, and Patrick reaches for my hand. Celia quirks her lips into a smile at the act, then focuses on the house up ahead.

Orange and yellow flames crawl out of the upstairs windows of the two-story house, daring the firemen to douse them. Clouds of black smoke plume from every crevice of the structure, as if it's weeping at its own destruction.

"Over there." Celia points.

I see Sean, his little sister, Penny, and his parents huddled together by the ambulance. Sean is doubled over coughing, and an EMT is trying to keep the oxygen mask on him. The house is engulfed in flames, snarling the message that it will not go down without a fight. When we get closer to the yard, a local policeman holds us at bay.

"Are you part of the family?" he asks.

I point at Penny. "She's my sister's best friend."

Surprisingly, these credentials seem to do just fine, and the officer lets us pass. Penny turns and sees me, her big black eyes shiny with tears. She breaks away from her mom, who is talking to a fireman, and comes over to us.

Bending down, I feel the need to hug her, and it looks like she needs it. "Penny, what happened?"

She shakes her head, her long hair flying. "I was upstairs. All I heard was Daddy screaming to get out of the house."

Sean and I make eye contact, and we head over to him. He's sitting on the back of the ambulance, covered in soot and smoke. Celia and I both hug him, and Penny cries even harder.

He lowers the oxygen mask and smiles at his little sister. "I'm okay, squirt."

This seems to placate the thirteen-year-old.

"What happened, Okra?" Celia asks. Since she's known him a lot longer than I have, she uses his nickname.

He shakes and scratches his head at the same time. "Dude, I was working on my physics assignment when something sparked in front of me and then . . ." He points to his burning house. "Then—this."

Celia the scientist takes over the questioning. "What exactly were you working on that would spark out of control?"

"That's just it," Sean says, gulping in air. "I wasn't using *anything* flammable. I don't understand what happened."

"Okra, tell me what kind of test it was."

"I was using litmus paper to test the acid levels in three different samples of water. And the whole damn thing just burst into flames in my hands, right there at the kitchen table."

I glance at Celia and then Patrick. Neither is buying it.

"That wouldn't cause an explosion," Patrick says.

"Are you sure you didn't put any sodium in the water that might have caused some sort of flare-up?" Celia presses.

"Honestly, Celia," Sean insists. "Litmus paper was the only thing I was working with."

One of the firemen walks up. "That's a very important question, son. You weren't using bleach or something that would promote a flame?"

Sean puts one hand on his heart and the other in a Boy Scout salute. "I swear on a thousand stacks of Bibles and on my grandmother's grave. Nothing but water."

"Yeah," I harrumph. "Water that ignited a destructive flame."

Patrick asks a question that's on the tip of my tongue. "Did you see anything, man? You know, anything out of the ordinary?"

Sean's dark eyes dart downward and he lifts the mask for another hit of the oxygen.

"Come on, Sean. You can tell us," I say. "We're ghost huntresses. We'll believe anything you tell us."

He laughs cynically. "Yeah, well, y'all won't believe this."

"Try us," I say.

"I swear, I saw that ugly-ass doll with the teddy bear from the fair exhibit. Standing right in the corner of the kitchen, laughing at me through the flames. That's not possible, right?" His eyes beg me to say it isn't.

I give him a halfhearted smile and say, "I'm afraid it might be."


A few hours later, Patrick's car is packed and we're standing in my driveway saying goodbye.

"This has been one hell of a weekend, huh?" he asks.

"Quite." I wrap my arms around him and lay my head on his chest. I hear his heartbeat ticking like a well-wound clock. "I hate that you have to leave."

He kisses the top of my head and cuddles me to him. "I'll be back Friday afternoon."

"I know. It's just there's so much weird shit going on."

"You've got your friends and fellow ghost huntresses here with you."

Celia, Becca, and Shelby-Nichole are sitting inside at my dining-room table waiting to tackle *whatever* it is that's going on. Just because I'm psychic doesn't mean I understand everything.

"Call me when you get home."

"You know I will."

I dig my bare toes into the pebbles of my driveway as I

watch the red taillights of Patrick's car disappear. I'm so glad he was here through the weekend while all this crap was going on. And more important, I'm grateful that he's on my side and patient with what I'm dealing with. Unlike someone I won't mention whose initials are Jason Tillson.

Back inside, I see that Mom has doled out lemonade and popcorn for the ghost huntresses. She's really come a long way in her belief in my abilities and in allowing me to investigate the paranormal.

For the next hour, we all sit at the table with our laptops, scouring the Internet, doing Google searches, and finding any information we can on that damned (literally) doll.

Celia rubs her eyes and laces her fingers together in front of her to stretch. Her knuckles pop, and Shelby-Nichole cringes.

"That is so not good for you."

Ignoring the chastising, Celia says, "The history on Xander is pretty much what we know already. It's cut-and-dried."

"Just like what Mr. Pfeiffer told us at the fair," Becca adds. "A present to the son from the slave nanny, Althea; after her death, strange things happened that were attributed to the doll."

"It doesn't add up," I chime in. "First Dragon's accident and the vision Patrick and I had of what he saw, and then the whole thing with Sean seeing Xander in his kitchen."

"Ooo! Look at this," Celia exclaims. "I found a website that has a collection of obituaries dating back to the eighteen hundreds."

"Eww, who'd want to be the webmaster of that site?" Shelby-Nichole asks.

"What is it?" I ask.

"A very short obit on Robert Townsend Farnsworth, who died in 1899 from an apparent suicide. Ate a bullet. The contents of his suicide note were never made public."

"That's creepy," Becca says. "Are you saying Xander the Doll killed him?"

"Who knows!" Celia says.

"Maybe it was something in the house plaguing him that he couldn't take anymore," I suggest.

Celia continues. "The first mention of the doll historically is when Farnsworth House and all of its contents became the property of the Radisson Historical Society. They used to have him in a chair in the main room back in the nineteen sixties and nineteen seventies, when they actually allowed visitors into the house. But there were too many complaints that Xander would go missing or would spook the visitors, so he was put upstairs in the room that used to be his. Even then, staff said he would relocate, thus his eventual encasement."

"So where does this thing about taking his picture come into play?" Becca asks.

"I asked Mr. Pfeiffer about this," Celia explains. "Sorry, forgot to tell you. It goes back to the sixties, when people would come to the house. Anyone who took a picture of Xander the Doll had something happen to them. A flat tire on the way home, illness from something they ate that day, a broken arm from a clumsy fall, you name it. Everything started getting attributed to Xander." Celia pauses for a moment. "You know, there's a tribe of indigenous people in Africa who believe if you take a picture of someone, you steal a part of his soul. I wonder if that's the case with Xander the Doll."

Becca snickers. "Dolls don't have souls, Celia."

I gnaw on the end of my index finger. "Maybe *this* one does."

"That's absurd," Shelby-Nichole says.

"We have to think of all possibilities."

"There is a legend that if you write an apology letter to Xander the Doll, your troubles will stop," Celia informs us. "Mr. Pfeiffer said they have a whole box of letters that they used to display . . . until they closed up the house."

"Why did they do that?" I ask.

"He wouldn't say."

"I don't understand why Xander the Doll has been so quiet all these years and is now striking out," Becca notes.

"Oh, the fair was his first appearance since 1999," Celia says.

I scrunch up my mouth and then let out a sigh. "It seems a history display may have unleashed an evil, unhappy entity that could be charming this doll."

Celia's eyes grow wide. "You may be right!"

"In any event, we've got to go on Facebook and look at all the pictures that were taken that night. We've got to warn everyone who snapped a picture with that damned doll."

———

At lunch the next day, Celia, Becca, and I are—strangely enough—sitting at the cheerleader table.

"How did you guys get sushi?" I ask, looking at the spread of California rolls, spicy tuna maki, and shrimp tempura that Stephanie and Farah have divided between them.

"Jim Roach does a co-op off campus two days a week, so I texted him our lunch order," Farah says with a laugh.

I glance across the caf to where Jim is sitting with his buddies Kyle and Sean and holding up a large piece of caterpillar sushi. Bleck . . . eel. That stuff is nasty.

Courtney Langdon picks at a salad with no dressing, and I'm just too upset to eat, although the turkey potpie I got does smell delish.

"How is Sean doing?" Celia asks.

Courtney looks over at him. "He's staying with Jim for the time being, but he's still majorly bummed. The house is pretty much ruined from top to bottom. What wasn't destroyed by smoke and fire has massive water damage."

Mr. and Mrs. Carmickle are staying in a hotel; their kids opted to stay with friends who offered them rooms. Like my parents did. Penny Carmickle is bunking with Kaitlin. I'm sure it'll help her heal from the fact that she just lost everything, including all of her precious video games that she and Kaitlin perfect every day after school.

"That sucks big-time," Becca says.

"His parents have awesome insurance though," Stephanie says between bites of spicy tuna roll. "The fire department said it had to be a wiring problem because of the age of the house. Sean said they're going to demolish it and build something brand-new with the insurance payout."

"At least something positive will come from it," Farah adds.

I stare at Farah. "It wasn't bad wiring in an old house. It was Xander the Doll. He is out for revenge."

Farah's eyes twinkle at me as she laughs hard. "Oh, Kendall, you're so cute with your psychic senses. You know I don't believe in any of those curses and stuff."

"Obviously," Celia says. "Since you were the one who snapped the pictures of the doll. Didn't you listen to Mr. Pfeiffer's stories of people who were cursed after that?"

"I did," Stephanie says.

"Me too," Courtney agrees.

Farah snickers. "Whatever. Pass the wasabi, Steph."

Frustrated, I lay my elbows on the table and shove my hands into my scalp, rubbing at the headache—a real one—that's developed as I try to get through to everyone.

"How do you explain what happened to Dragon?" Becca says.

"Maybe he hit an oil patch," Farah suggests.

"Maybe something distracted him and freaked him out," Celia says. "And what about Sean's house? Bursting into flames from testing water with litmus paper? I don't think so. That's not how it works."

Courtney's face becomes ashen. "Y'all, we should listen to them. They know their stuff."

"Tru' dat," Stephanie says.

Rolling her eyes, Farah asks, "What am I supposed to do to remove this alleged curse?"

"You need to write a letter of apology to Xander the Doll."

She waves a chopstick at us dismissively. "I love y'all and I know you're, like, all into the paranormal and stuff, but I don't believe it." She uses her chopsticks to emphasize her points. "First off, I have a paper on Lord Byron due Monday, my opera recital is Saturday—and I have the lead solo—and I have to get my nails done." Farah puts down the chopsticks and spreads her fingers for emphasis.

I've never heard anyone who can sing like Farah. She's like an opera diva at seventeen. But that doesn't excuse the fact that she toyed with something dark and refuses to deal with it.

"You've got to do it, Farah," Celia begs.

"I don't have time, hon."

"Everyone who took a picture with Xander the Doll has had something bad befall them," I say with great passion in my voice. "Dragon, Sean . . ."

"Not Jim," Farah says.

At that precise moment, across the caf, there's a horrendous clamor around Jim Roach's table. Roachie stands up and grabs at his throat, coughing and gagging while his face turns beet red.

"Someone help!" Kyle screams out. "He's choking!"

"Oh my God!" Courtney yells.

"I don't know the Heimlich, do you?" I ask Celia and Becca.

Both shake their heads.

Roachie's face is getting redder and redder and he's trying to breathe.

Chaos ensues in the lunchroom as people run around trying to help. Lucas Hesse, a football player, tries to hoist Jim up from behind, but he's not doing it right. He's only making matters worse.

Then I hear laughter over the screaming and yelling. A squeaky high laugh with a disturbing tone to it. I swear it must be Xander the Doll. He's here. Out of his case. He. Is. Here.

One of the lunch ladies pushes everyone aside and comes to Jim's rescue. She laces her hands around his middle and gives the heave-ho several times, finally dislodging the wedged sushi. Jim collapses onto the table, huffing and puffing, gasping in the precious air.

I turn steely eyes on Farah. "You were saying?"

"I didn't even do anything and I'm going to write a letter," Stephanie says. She had previously been the victim of some pretty nasty paranormal activity that threatened her house and her home life.

"Me too," Courtney says. "We'll do it at study hall."

"Fine . . . whatever," Farah says. She turns to Stephanie. "Write the letter and sign my name to it as well. I'll be on the computer researching Lord Byron. Someone who actually existed and something I'm being graded on." She gathers up the remnants of her lunch and snags her giant Coach bag. "And, y'all, don't forget my recital Saturday. I'm doing an aria from *Madama Butterfly* and I totally rock."

I smile at her, somewhat relieved. "I'd love to come. And I'll bring my boyfriend."

"You do that," Farah says. "He's a cutie."

Shelby-Nichole stops by the table before Farah leaves. "Hey, y'all. Remember we're doing yearbook group pics on Friday. We'll do individual ones as well."

"I'll e-mail the squad a reminder of what uniform to wear," Courtney says.

"Awesome," Shelby-Nichole says. "Oh, and Kendall, I'll need your help after school today."

"Sure thing."

Good.

Something to keep my mind off the mayhem going on around me.

Hopefully the apology letter to Xander will be enough to appease him.

# CHAPTER ELEVEN

AFTER SCHOOL, I GO TO DIVINING WOMAN to do some readings and talk to Loreen.

Stephanie Crawford texted me that she and Courtney wrote the apology letter to Xander the Doll, and the two of them signed it, as did Farah. Actually, Farah had Stephanie sign her name. Hopefully that'll be enough.

Time for work. I'm not exactly in the mood to read other people's futures right now, but folks count on me. I close my eyes, surround myself in God's protective white light, and get down to business.

Mrs. Harmon from the yarn store is worried about whether a large mole on her back is cancerous. I'm psychic, not a doctor, and I would never give advice about such a deadly disease.

"You need to call your doctor and have it looked at," I say to her, stacking the tarot cards and refusing to make a medical diagnosis. "He's the one who will have answers for you."

She widens her eyes like this is the smartest thing she's ever heard. "Why, Kendall, you're so intuitive. I'll call the doctor tomorrow."

She pays Loreen twenty dollars at the register and leaves a five-dollar tip for me.

I feel like a charlatan taking a tip for something so obvious; I just told her what any normal person would have.

Then Morgan Brown from the flower shop sits down opposite me wanting a reading. She is worried that her boyfriend will never propose to her, and she's inching toward the conclusion of her childbearing years. She wants the cards to tell her if and when it will happen or whether she should break up with him. With my psychic vision I can see that the owner of the Michelin tire store, Jaden Spees, has been saving up money to get Morgan a ring. I don't want to ruin his surprise, but in the meantime, I need her to not scare him away.

"Your relationship is very solid. You can't push things."

Morgan is quite impatient. "Excuse my French, Kendall, but Jaden needs to either shit or get off the pot."

"Morgan!" Loreen calls out to her.

"Well, it's true! I arrange flowers for everyone's wedding in this town. I want to be the bride. I want to be a wife and mother. I need it to be my turn."

"It will be," I say to her. "You just have to be patient, and don't put any pressure on him, just enjoy being together. When the time is right, it'll happen."

November 25, to be exact, although I'm not telling her that for all the tea in China.

The smile on her face shows her satisfaction, and she too pays and leaves a tip.

When she exits the store, I collapse on the couch in the back.

"Your aura is horrible today, Kendall," Loreen comments. "You can't take on everyone's problems as your own."

The longest sigh in history escapes from me.

"Talk to me. I'm here to listen."

I spill everything to Loreen about Xander the Doll, all that's been happening, and my overwhelming sense of impending doom.

"You can't stop what's already been set in motion, Kendall."

"I know," I say, somewhat exasperated. "It's so hard when you have intuition but people won't listen to you."

She nods. "It's not much different than a mother looking out for a child. No matter how much she cares for him or protects him, a child is going to do what he wants. The universe has a plan for all of us and a reason for everything."

I scowl. "So the universe had a plan to crash Dragon's bike, burn down Sean's house, and try to choke Jim Roach to death?"

"I'm only saying that it's all part of the bigger plan and we can't know what that is right now. It's not in our power. Even for those who are sensitive, like us."

"Loreen, for the most part I believe that. I just can't accept that these things were meant to be, especially when all of these people say they saw Xander the Doll when these events happened. I mean, even Jim saw him in the cafeteria."

"Oh, you didn't tell me that."

"Yes, he told Sean that he saw Xander the Doll in the

lunchroom. I've been seeing him everywhere, Loreen. I believe in this curse. I've seen too much in my short time in Radisson to *not* believe that the stories of him are true. I just want to know what I can do to stop him before someone gets hurt worse, or killed."

She comes over, sits with me, and gives me a hug. "You'll do what you have to do." She pulls two fives and a twenty out of her pocket and hands them to me. "Your take for the day. Go home and get some rest. Meditate and pray for guidance."

It's the best advice I've gotten in a long time.

Wearily, I park my car in the driveway. Mom and Dad are both still at work, so maybe I can get in a good nap before dinner is served.

I walk toward the back porch, where big, fat Natalie is cleaning her black fur in the sunshine. I bend down and scratch her behind her kitty ears. Her long pink tongue continues to wipe at her fur and then at my hand. The purr that motors out from her is the best sound I've heard all day.

"Does the pretty girl want to come in and take a nap with me?"

Natalie's green eyes look up at me as if she actually under-stands. She yawns profusely, her pink mouth opening wide enough for me to see all of her teeth.

"Come on, sweetie," I say to her.

She stands up, arching her back as she stares past me.

"What do you see, girl?"

The sweetest kitty in the world then shows her claws and hisses something fierce. I think she's hissing at me until I realize something is behind me. Not another animal, and neither of her cat siblings, Eleanor or Buckley. Something ominous and threatening—to her, to me. I slowly turn, but there's no one there. The hairs on my arms are standing at attention as I watch Natalie leap forward and swat her claws at nothing.

"What do you see, Natty?"

More hissing and a loud meow that echoes through the neighborhood.

I focus my energies on the spot where she's involved in this altercation. I don't see him, but I know Xander the Doll is there. Or was there. His essence fills my nostrils. The odor of musty fabric is present in the air.

Natalie leaps forward. I jump back.

"Is that you, Xander?"

Nothing.

*Meeeeeeeow! Raaaaarrrrrrr . . .*

"Leave me and my friends alone, Xander."

Natalie rears up on her hind legs and whacks the air again.

"Leave my cat alone!"

The air shifts and suddenly it's freezing cold in the middle of April in Georgia. I breathe out a sigh, and I can see the icy trail of my condensated breath. Okay, so that's probably not a real word, but it works here.

"Whoever or whatever is possessing this doll, I can help. Just show yourself to me."

Nothing.

*Rarrrrrrrrr . . . hissssssssssss . . .*

I reach down and scoop Natty into my arms, not wanting to deal with what might be out here. I've made my offer. The next move is Xander's.

I go through the back door of the house, drop Natalie on the floor next to her bowl of Iams, and toss my book bag and purse on the kitchen table. Before I can grab an ice-cold Diet Coke out of the fridge, Penny Carmickle runs up to me with the cordless phone in her hand. Like I said, she's staying with us for a few days while her parents are dealing with the insurance payments and everything. Two Kaitlins in the house. Lucky me.

"It's for you, Kendall."

Now what?

Is Xander on the phone?

Or, worse—is it the haunted-sandwich man? I'm too tired to deal with anyone right now, particularly the haunted-sandwich man. He e-mailed again last night, saying the sandwich was now following his son to school and making him act up in class.

I wave Penny off and whisper, "Take a message . . . I'm not here."

She frowns deeply at me. "I already told the woman you were here."

A woman?

I take the receiver and smile into it, knowing clearly now who's on the end of the line. "This is Kendall."

"Hi, Kendall, it's Andrea Caminiti."

"Yeah, I know."

She laughs quietly. "That's right. You're psychic."

"So they tell me," I say, trying to recover from the altercation—if you can call it that—outside. "How are you?"

Andi pauses a moment, then says, "I'm fine. We're still waiting for those DNA results, you know."

"Yes, ma'am. I'm eager to see what they say."

"Me too," she says. She clears her throat and then adds, "I wanted to reach out to you, Kendall. I had a dream about you the other night. You were in Italy."

"Really?" I say, my mouth dropping open. "I've had a psychic vision that my maternal grandparents are in Italy. John Thomas and Anna Wynn Faulkner. Emily Jane Faulkner's parents. Does the name mean *anything* to you?" I implore.

I can see Andi sitting in her studio, on the couch, nervously bouncing her heeled foot on her crossed knee. "Actually," she starts, "I never knew her full name."

"Oh, Andi! Why didn't you tell me before?"

"I'm still a bit shaken by you, Kendall."

"Please tell me everything you know," I beg, gripping the phone tightly.

"It's not much," Andi says. "My brother met her in English lit class. They both had a love and appreciation of Shakespeare."

That makes sense, since Celia and I are always quoting the Bard.

"Andy told me there was a beautiful girl from his class who

worked at the diner off campus. He'd go in to study—and check her out—and she'd bring him complimentary chocolate fudge sundaes. Sometimes they would share it."

"Aww . . . that's so sweet." I can completely see Emily being all nurturing. Especially to someone she was so in love with. That I'm sure of.

"He didn't tell me much. Which was odd, because he told me about every girl he hooked up with in high school," Andi says. "Because he wouldn't talk much about Emily, I knew she was special. That for him, she was the one."

I visualize a matronly woman with perfectly coifed hair, pearls, and a wrinkle-free Chanel suit. She looks posh. She looks rich. She looks disappointed.

I swallow hard and ask, "Your mother didn't approve of Emily, did she?"

There's a gasp. "How did you—oh, right . . ."

I take a seat at the kitchen table instead of continuing to pace around. "You can tell me, Andi."

"From what Mother knew of Emily and her family, she thought Emily was below him, because of her humble background and that she was in college on work-study and student aid."

"So he never brought her to visit?"

"No. Although if what you say is true, that they died in a car accident together, they may have been coming to St. Louis during their Christmas break."

I gnaw on my bottom lip. "And since Emily was pregnant—

with me—it may not have been a very merry Christmas had they made it."

"We'll never know, will we, Kendall?"

"I'm certainly trying to find out," I say.

Andi clears her throat again. "I don't even have any pictures of them together. But I do know one thing. My brother was very much in love with her."

Her brother . . . possibly my father. Both of them taken away from me before I was even in the world. What would my life have been like these past seventeen years? Either I'd have been raised by a single mom because Andy Caminiti's family didn't approve of her and me, or I would have had very happily in-love young parents struggling to take care of me. I realize that my ending up adopted by the Mooreheads was a true blessing in disguise. I may not have had my genetic parents, but there's been no shortage of food, clothing, shelter, and, most of all, love.

"That's nice to hear," I say finally. "Well, Emily *was* my birth mother; that's a fact."

"I understand," Andi says.

Shifting the phone to my other ear, I add, "I think it would be cool to have you as an aunt."

Andrea Caminiti lets out a lengthy sigh' and then says, "Thank you."

We both sit there a moment taking everything in. An emotional knot in my throat threatens to choke me up, but I gulp it down deep, not wanting to cry. I know that on the other end of the phone, Andi is feeling her own overwhelmedness. Her own bubbling emotions over the loss of her brother and the— dare I say?—hope that he has left a legacy. Me, I just want to know who I am.

"I should let you go, Kendall. I'm sure you've got home- work to do."

I think of that #$%^ing history paper I haven't worked on. "That I do." Then I feel compelled to say, "Thanks for calling. You made my day."

"I'll let you know when I receive our results. Goodbye, Kendall."

I click off the phone and return it to the cradle. The call was brief but meaningful. I sense a close connection with the woman who is so far away from me.

I can't wait for the DNA results.

## Chapter Twelve

FRIDAY AT SCHOOL is cahhhhrazzzeeee!

Mr. Rorek gives us a pop quiz on the Battle of Gettysburg—thank heavens I finally read the chapters and watched the *Gettysburg* movie torrent Patrick downloaded for me—and Mr. Duncan tests our knowledge of metaphors, similes, and parallelism. I wasn't prepared to have so much demanded of me on a Friday. It's like all the teachers are out to get us and work our collective arse off. On top of the academic stuff, I've got all of my yearbook duties. Girlfriend needs a long soak in a hot tub to recover from this school day.

"Everyone say *crack-a-lack*," Celia says as she poses in the front row of the science club for their yearbook picture.

*Snap. Snap. Snap.*

Shelby-Nichole has got literally everyone on staff—even us ad people—taking pictures. Today all of the clubs and organizations are on the docket for their group shots. I'm not that bad at the whole photography thing. I mean, it's digital, how can I mess up? Just get everyone in the frame and click.

I have permission to skip the last two periods of the day to help out with all the yearbook pandemonium. So far, I've snapped the pep club pepping, the glee club gleeing, the drama club being dramatic, and now Celia's club . . . being scientific. First we did a pose in the biology lab with all of them holding up beakers and test tubes and such. Shelby-Nichole complimented our creativity but also wanted a more serious posed group shot. She's the boss!

Just as I'm finishing up with the science club, Shelby-Nichole rushes into the library where one of the makeshift photo studios has been set up. She clutches her clipboard and adjusts her glasses on the bridge of her nose.

"Kendall, I've had to switch things around a little bit. Ashley Whittier had to leave early to go to the doctor, so I need you to fill in for her." She lowers her voice to a whisper. "She thinks she has some kind of infection."

A disturbing flash of information crosses my mind. "Actually, it's a urinary tract infection," I say without hesitation. Oops. There I go doing medical diagnosis. Honestly, at times I wish these visions wouldn't provide me with so much detail. When I do want to know more, it's like the visions are few and far between. "Umm . . . I think that's what's wrong with her."

Shelby-Nichole giggles at me. "That's, like, TMI, but in any case, I need you to take her last shoot, if you don't mind."

Patrick texted me earlier that he had to do something with his dad this afternoon and won't be here in Radisson until dinnertime, so I have time to kill.

"Anything to help out," I say with a cheesy grin.

"Awesome. I need you to go down to the football field and get pics of the varsity cheerleaders. We need a group pose, one or two pyramid pictures, and individual shots of each girl."

I mock salute her and raise the camera to my heart. "Aye, aye, Chief."

This is good. I like being busy with regular teenage things. Less time to listen to the voices in my head that want to lure me into yet another mystery of this haunted town I live in. I'm glad to have the yearbook work as a distraction, and a focus. Father Mass was smart telling me to get involved with something at school. Everyone needs to be well-rounded, and I certainly need the hobby. Plus, I'm helping out, participating in extracurricular activities, and making new friends outside of my ghost hunting. Even my former nemesis Courtney Langdon is speaking to me like I'm a normal human being. I guess these things just take time.

It's a ten-minute walk to go all the way from the library, through the school complex, past the gym and the baseball field and the parking lot, and down the concrete steps of Arnold Claude Bassett Stadium, our home football field. None of the girls are there yet, so I open the field gate and cross over to the south goalpost, where I think we'll set up the group shot.

As I'm positioning the tripod and screwing the camera into place, the cheerleaders start arriving in their white sleeveless uniforms with the red-and-black-lettered *RHS* on the front and the pleated white skirt. They look all happy and peppy and cheerleadery. I admire them for putting themselves out there in front of the crowds during football and basketball season, doing dance routines, cheers, and gymnastics. Me, I'd fall off the top of the pyramid and break every bone in my body if I tried to do what they do.

"Hey, Kendall!" Stephanie Crawford calls out. She waves a red and white pompom at me. "Cool! You're taking our pics today?"

"I am indeed."

"Awesome. Make sure you take my good side. À la Mariah Carey."

I laugh as I knuckle bump her pompommed hand. "Your spring-break tan really stands out with that white outfit."

She does a little twirly-twirl for me. "It does, doesn't it? I'm going to have to do the tanning bed to keep it until summer kicks in."

Several of the other girls arrive, checking their hair in makeup mirrors and touching up their mascara, lipstick, and powder.

Courtney shows up carrying the school's spirit bear, spirit sticks, and a megaphone, along with her pompoms. Even though Courtney and I got off to a bad start, I can totally see why Jason Tillson went for her. She's really beautiful, with her flowing blond hair and sparkling eyes. She seems to have mellowed out the bitchiness since her spirit oppression and now mainly concentrates on spirit of the school-pride kind.

"Over here, girls," she orders. Then she turns to me. "You're our photog today?"

"Hope that's okay," I say with a weak smile.

"You'll do in a pinch." Then we smile at each other. I'm so grateful that her Mean Girl days are done.

"Oh, y'aaall! You're kidding me?" I hear from behind. We all turn to see Farah Lewis running up to us. She's not late, but she's wearing the wrong uniform. It's the exact replica of what the others have on, only it's the *red* version, not the white one. "No! No, I didn't. I wore the wrong friggin' uniform?"

Courtney throws her hands up in disgust. "Farah, didn't you get the e-mail I sent out to everyone? I said the home white uniform." She rolls her eyes for emphasis.

Farah smacks her head. "Oh my God. I'm so sorry. I've been concentrating so much on my recital and practicing my songs; I thought the red uniform was the home one."

"Do we need to reschedule?" Courtney asks me.

I scrunch up my nose. "The yearbook team is working over the weekend to get the layout finished and shipped to the printer. We really need all of the club and organizational photos done today." I shift my eyes to Farah's red outfit. "Maybe Shelby-Nichole can Photoshop it to be white?"

"If that's what we have to do," Courtney says.

"No, no, no. I don't want to cause extra work for anyone." Farah drops her pompoms and gym bag to the field. "Don't worry. I live like fifteen minutes from school. I'll run home and get the right uniform and we can do the group pictures last."

Stephanie and Courtney exchange looks. "That'll work," Courtney says. "Does that work for you, Kendall?"

It's no big deal. Besides, I want to do the girls justice with good pictures that don't need to be doctored. "No worries," I say.

Farah grabs her purse and tugs out her keys. "I'll be right back."

"Don't speed!" Stephanie yells.

Farah waves, dashes across the field, and runs back up the steps.

"Okay, then," I say, taking charge. "Fourteen girls to snap. Let's start with the individual pictures."

Courtney goes first, of course. We decided to get about eight pics of each girl. She stands sideways with her left leg pulled up to the knee of her right, and her poms on her hips. Next, she's lying on her stomach on the field with her legs crossed at the ankles in the air behind her. Totally cute and such a cheerleader pic. I get a couple of her doing jumps. Those turn out really well, so others decide they'll do that too.

One by one, I click away pictures of the team. Lauren Abbot even does a split for her picture. Ouch, ouch, ouch! No, thank you!

But I'm having a great time and this is a lot of fun. I can totally see why Taylor was so addicted to the way the world looked from behind the lens. My heart aches momentarily when I think of my friend. I miss her a ton and I don't hear from her often enough. Sure, we e-mail the occasional joke, and we IM'd when she first left town, but it's not the same. I hope she'll come back to Radisson this summer to at least visit. Mom told me that Mrs. Tillson is out of rehab and back at home with her sister. Of course, if Taylor comes back to town, that means . . .

I shake myself out of the reverie and get back to the task at hand. Jason Tillson is out of my life. Right now, I'm a yearbook photographer and I need to concentrate on delivering the best pictures that I can. It'll be cool to look at the annual one day and know that I helped out in such a tangible way. I mean, selling ads to help us pay for the printing is one thing. This is something that I can point to and say, *I did that.*

Twenty minutes later and ten girls down, I relish the jolt of energy rushing through me. "Next victim," I call out with a chortle.

"That would be me," Stephanie says.

"Awesome!"

She reaches over to her left wrist and unhooks her watch, laying it next to her purse. "It's been a half-hour," she says. "I wonder where Farah is."

"She'll be back," Courtney states. "She better be, or you *will* have to Photoshop her."

Stephanie ignores her captain and stands in front of my camera. Her long, gold-brown hair is pulled into her signature side ponytail, and her makeup is flawless. She mimics the poses

Courtney did, foot up, lying in the grass, and then she does a cutesy little squat pose with her elbow on her knee and her chin resting on her fist.

"That's a great one," I say, clicking away. "Do you want to do some jump shots now?"

"Let me stretch for a second."

I take that time to switch out the SD memory card in the camera and then turn back to Stephanie.

"Ready?"

"Yeah, just a sec," she says.

Then my vision begins to blur. Is it from the heat and all the running around I've been doing? I stand up straight and rub hard at my eyes. Ack . . . I hope I'm not developing myopia or anything. The haziness isn't clearing no matter how hard I blink. Then the clouds start rolling in, dropping a hazy film across the football stadium. This is so inconvenient. Just when I'm almost done with the shoot. The headache begins tapping at my temples and I know this isn't good.

*Oh no . . .*

There is no mist. At least, not really. Not one that nonpsychic people can see.

In the mist is danger. A confusion that I can't suss out.

"Kendall, are you all right?" Stephanie calls to me. I hear her through the screen of fog and reach out with my hands. Nothing is there. Everything has faded away into nothingness. I squint, trying to focus in the distance. I close my eyes hard. I reopen them. The murky miasma remains, creeping toward me on determined feet.

"Kendall?"

But no one can help me. I'm deep into the vision. I'm absorbed in the moisture and steam around me pulling me closer and closer. The wind howls a sad, sad song, almost crying with the message it has to bring to me. This is more than something in my eyes or my tiredness from taking so many pictures. It's a deep trance that's sucking me farther and farther down into the abyss.

*Help me,* I call out.

There isn't anyone to hear me.

The cheerleaders are gone and I'm on my own, swatting away the flies of confusion soaring around, nipping at me, and buzzing so close to my ears.

I'm helpless in this deep chasm, struggling to escape.

*Just show me what you need to and let me go,* I beg whoever is presenting me with this.

It can't be good. Nothing this trancey ever is.

A figure forms in the distance, dark and shadowed in a silhouette of smoke. It's . . . oh no . . . it's Anona.

*Why are you doing this to me?*

She nearly floats to me in a cloud tinged with silver and blue, shining through the murky darkness. Her lips part and she whispers her warning.

*It is happening again . . .*

*Then stop it!* I scream out.

*No one can stop it . . .*

*You have to!*

A bloodcurdling screech peals from my throat. One that could strip paint from the side of a house. My body spirals out of control, falling . . . falling . . . falling . . .

From above my body, I see Stephanie, Courtney, and Lauren run to my aid. I'm on the ground; my camera is two feet away. Why won't Anona help me? Why can't she stop whatever is happening? Why can't I? Why tell me if there's nothing I can do?

As I'm lying helpless on the ground, searing pain blazes right through me like it's my own. My chest is heavy, my lungs filling with blood, my organs caving in, much like when my lung collapsed after my accident. Only this isn't an accident that I'm part of; I'm only feeling it. Someone else is experiencing it for real. Every breath is a chore I don't have the strength to complete. The throbbing is so intense, so hot. Tears rain from my eyes, nearly enough to irrigate the football field. I can't speak. Words are clogged with nowhere to go.

My neck snaps—just like hers.

My bones are crushed—just like hers.

The sounds of a heart fighting to survive—then nothing.

"Help her!" I yell. "Oh, God! Someone please help her!"

No one can help her.

Certainly not me.

And I black out.

# CHAPTER THIRTEEN

FARAH LEWIS'S TWISTED VOLKSWAGEN Jetta was found wrapped around the large elm tree at the corner of Exeter Street and Highway 16, just one mile from her house. It was next to the jackknifed semi that seems to have skidded over to her side of the road before ending up in the ditch.

From what the authorities can make out, in her rush to get home and pick up the correct cheerleader uniform, she didn't notice the truck taking its turn at the four-way stop. Too late, Farah swerved to miss the oncoming eighteen-wheeler. Her car skidded into the brush and hit the tree head on.

The paramedics pronounced the seventeen-year-old cheer-leader and budding opera singer dead at the scene. Although it appeared that she had put her seat belt on, the police said it looked like it came undone at some point. She was thrown into the steering wheel, and it crushed her chest and snapped her neck.

The level of pain, hurt, confusion, and sadness I'm feeling is beyond devastating. I literally saw the wreck as it was occur-ring. As. It. Was. Happening. There was nothing I could have done to warn her or to stop it from happening. What the hell good are these psychic visions if I can't *prevent* horrible things from taking place?

I sit on my bed, numb from head to toe. Patrick is next to me, rubbing my back and shoulders, trying to soothe my ache.

I sip air into my lungs, no longer crying out in empathy from what Farah experienced in her last minutes. My tears stream down my face, wetting my black blouse in fat splotches.

"Get it out, Kendall." Patrick's voice is tender and caring.

"Poor Farah," I say in between sobs. "Poor, beautiful Farah with the voice of an angel. It's so not fair."

Patrick rubs my hair. "Now she can sing *with* the angels."

It's Monday morning and Radisson High School is closed due to the tragedy. Patrick got permission to skip school in Duluth so he could be here with me today. "I wasn't best friends with Farah, but she was a very nice person. She didn't deserve to die so young. I don't understand."

"There are things in this world people aren't meant to understand, Kendall. Even psychics like us."

Mom raps lightly on the door and I lift my eyes. "Celia and Becca are downstairs. Are you two ready to go?"

I stand and lean on my bureau. My eyes are bloodshot from three days of crying. There's really no use in trying to wear makeup when it'll just end up on the tissues I have crammed into my purse. I smooth my hand over my black skirt, one I borrowed from Mom. I reach into my jewelry box and pull out my Grandma Ethel's crystal necklace, feeling that I want a connection with the one other person I knew who died. Then I grab my sunglasses and perch them on my head.

Patrick follows me out the bedroom door and down the stairs to where Celia and Becca are waiting. Of course, Becca has no shortage of black clothing, but somehow she seems more demure today. Celia wears a black blazer, a gray shirt, and black dress pants. She sort of looks as if she's going on a job interview, and it makes me smile.

"Hey, y'all," Becca says. "Ready to go?"

"As ready as I'll ever be for something like this."

Celia wraps her arm around my shoulder and walks on my left; Patrick is on my right. I don't know why everyone is handling me with such kid gloves. Yeah, I realize the whole varsity cheerleading squad witnessed my freak-out, my collapse, and then my blackout, but I'm still alive. I'm not the one we're eulogizing today.

This is a huge deal for the sleepy little town of Radisson, Georgia. The police have the street in front of the United Methodist church blocked off, and they're directing traffic for the many funeral-goers.

"There must be a couple hundred people here," Celia mutters when we walk up.

"I can't believe it," I say in a whisper.

When we get to the front of the church, an usher stops us.

"Are you close friends or family?"

Becca cops an attitude. "Umm, yeah, we went to school with her."

He drums his fingers together. "It's just that we barely have enough seats in the church to hold everyone. If you're not immediate friends or family, I'm going to have to ask you to go to the fellowship hall and watch the service from the video feed."

Stephanie Crawford walks out of the sanctuary, past the usher, and puts her arm around me. She's wearing the all-black cheerleader uniform with *RHS* in red and white lettering that I've seen at basketball games. I'd heard that the cheerleaders were serving as pallbearers, but I had no idea they would be in mourning uniforms.

"Mr. Abramson," she says sweetly, "Kendall, Celia, and Becca are very good friends and they should be shown into the church. Patrick too."

We all nod our thanks and run the gauntlet into the place of worship.

RHS students, faculty, and administrators fill the right side of the church; Farah's family and other friends are on the left. The four of us slip into the sixth row and sit close together so others can fill in.

Farah's class picture sits in a frame on the altar, surrounded by candles, stuffed animals, cards, and flowers. Her casket—closed—is a simple one of white steel with shiny silver handles. A blanket of pink roses and baby's breath cover it, with her *white* cheerleader uniform draped over the top.

"That damned uniform," I snarl through my teeth.

"We're in church, Kendall," Celia fusses.

"It's because of that uniform that she's dead."

Celia takes my hand and squeezes it, trying to empathize. But no one other than Patrick can understand the pain I'm experiencing. The intense pressure on my vital organs is palpable.

Tears slip from the corners of my eyes. "We should have just Photoshopped it. Why did I let her leave?"

"It's not your fault, Kendall," Patrick murmurs to me. "Stop beating yourself up. It was her time."

My eyes shoot to Patrick's. "How can it be a seventeen-year-old's time? I do *not* understand that."

"Shhh," Becca says from the other side of Celia. "The music's starting."

The RHS cheerleaders lead the processional and sit on the right side of the church in the front rows. Farah's family follows—her mother and father, holding hands, and her two little sisters, one near Kaitlin's age and the other looking about nine at the most. My heart goes out to them over their loss. They'll never hear Farah sing again or watch her do backflips at pep rallies.

I sniff into the Kleenex I retrieve from my purse. Patrick snuggles me into the crook of his arm, and the service begins.

Strangely enough, even though this is a funeral for one so young, there's a celebratory atmosphere. The sanctuary is filled with the sweetness of freshly bloomed flowers of all sizes, shapes, and colors. The minister follows the family in, climbs to the altar, and then leads us in prayer. As soon as he's done, Farah's mother steps to the pulpit. She's wearing a charcoal gray suit that hugs her curves, and she sports an almost vibrant smile.

"Farah loved life. And she lived every moment of her life to the fullest. She loved singing and she loved dancing and she loved cheerleading. She loved her friends and she was so looking forward to her future and applying to the Berklee College of Music in Boston to pursue her opera career. That was cut short when our precious girl lost control of her car . . ." Mrs. Lewis stops for a moment to dab her eye with a tissue. She continues though. "Farah would be the first to say, 'Mom, don't have a boring old funeral for me. It should be a party.'"

We all laugh, and I can actually imagine Farah saying that.

Mrs. Lewis smiles through her tears. "She would have wanted us to remember her laughing, cheering, and singing. So this will be a celebration of her short life. In honor of my daughter's memory, the choir will sing several of her favorite songs. Thank you all for being here and for loving Farah almost as much as we did."

The organ hums to life and the choir begins singing "Ave Maria." The soloist steps forward to perform the classic piece, and I close my eyes to absorb the loveliness of the aria.

"Oh my God," I hear. "That woman is, like, totally butchering this masterpiece."

Slowly, I peel open my eyes and see Farah—or rather, the ghost of her—sitting on the bench in front of me. She's wearing her red cheerleader uniform and turns back to talk to me, rolling her eyes in the process.

"What are you doing here?" I lean forward and whisper.

Celia and Becca twist to look at me, so I sit back into the seat.

Farah looks exactly the same as she did when I saw her leave the football field in search of the correct uniform. Thank heavens she's not appearing to me bloody and battered from her accident. I totally couldn't take that.

"Ugh!" Farah says. "I appreciate the effort, but that woman has *no* business trying to hit those high notes. *No one* hits a high C like I do."

"I agree with you," I whisper.

Patrick nudges me to be quiet, but I nod to indicate where Farah is sitting. He shrugs, which tells me he doesn't see her.

*It's Farah. She's right here.*

*I can't see her.*

*Well, I can.*

I speak to her in my mind so I won't disrupt the service.

*Do you know the state of your being?* I ask in my head.

"Duh," she says with a giggle. "I'm, like, dead, Kendall. No one could have lived through *that* accident." She cranes her neck to see the casket and then slumps back in the seat. "Closed casket, huh? Damn. I wanted to see what outfit Mom put on me."

*I'll find out,* I say in my head.

With clear astonishment, Farah twists in the pew and hangs over the back of it, staring at me with amazement. "Oh my God! You really *can* see the dead, Kendall. That is soooooooo cool."

*It's not cool that you're dead, Farah.*

She waves me off with her hand. "I never knew so many people cared about me."

*Of course they do. See the turnout today? There's even a video feed for people in the fellowship hall.*

Her white teeth sparkle as she smiles. "Seriously? Yet I couldn't get nominated for homecoming court this past fall. Explain that to me."

I try to suppress my laughter, but it trickles out. I clear my throat over it so no one thinks I'm full of hilarity at a funeral, even if it has been termed a life celebration.

At least Farah recognizes that she's passed and isn't one of these moody-ass ghosts that I've dealt with. But . . .

*Why haven't you passed into the light?* I ask her in my head.

She curls her lip and her eyes blaze out at me. "I don't know. I think I have something I have to do before I leave."

*Like what?*

"I'm supposed to lead you somewhere, but I just don't know where yet. I'm going to poke around town and I'll let you know." She pauses for a moment, and I fear she might disappear on me. Then she adds, "I know one thing. I've got to even the score."

*What score? What are you talking about?*

Her finger pointing, Farah says, "I want to get even with the damned doll."

*Doll? Are you telling me Xander the Doll caused this?*

"Oh yeah," she starts. "I was driving just fine—okay, I was

speeding a little bit—and that *thing* appeared out of nowhere right in front of my car. That's why I swerved. I thought it was a real little kid and there was no way I was going to mow down a child. Then I heard the creepy thing laughing at me before I slammed into that tree."

*I've heard the laughter too,* I tell her.

"He completely messed me up. It's bad enough that my precious Jetta is going to the scrap pile, but I missed the recital on Saturday and now . . ." She spreads out her hands. "Well, now I'm like this."

*I'm so sorry you died, Farah. I told you to write the apology letter to Xander.*

"Yeah, Steph and Court did it and forged my name. I couldn't be bothered with it because I didn't believe it. But, Kendall, I *saw* and *heard* him. He took pleasure in killing me! I want to see him pay."

I nod my head vehemently at her. *I do too. He's hurt too many people. This has to end.*

Farah smiles at me. "So you'll help me, right? I mean, like, you're really psychic and all. You'll know how to fix this, won't you?"

Her beautiful eyes implore me.

How can I not help?

I don't care what anyone else thinks or believes about this evil, enchanted devil of a doll. I'm going after him. And I'm going to make sure he never harms anyone again.

## Chapter Fourteen

Patrick and I walk back to the house after the service, leaving Becca and Celia to fend for themselves. It's not that I don't want to share Farah's visit with them ... just not right now. I need to let it soak in.

"I shouldn't be surprised that Farah came to you," Patrick says.

I nod. "Could you hear me talking to her?"

"Only your side of the convo, strangely enough."

We cross Delmonico Street and walk over to Main in silence. Patrick swings our joined hands back and forth as I kick a rock along our path. The sun shines hot overhead, and I'm starting to sweat in my funeral clothes. All I want to do is strip down to shorts and a tank and lie under the ceiling fan in my room and ... not think.

But I have to think. Farah Lewis is stuck in some sort of limbo because she has to lead me somewhere, and I need to help her find peace.

We walk into my yard, go past my mother's flower garden,

and step up onto the front porch. I take a seat on the swing, and Patrick sits next to me.

"What does she want you to do?" Patrick asks.

"She wants to get even with Xander the Doll."

Patrick sighs hard. "*Him* again?"

"Yep. She saw him and that's what caused her to swerve." I fill Patrick in on everything Farah said to me during the service.

Patrick's brown eyes darken and he glowers a bit. "We've got to help her cross."

"Tell me something I don't know. There's even more. She says she can't leave until she helps me. That there's someplace I have to be shown." I rub my head. "I'm so confused, Patrick."

"We'll figure it out together," he says.

Tilting forward, I prop my elbows on my thighs and squiggle my hands into my hair, rubbing hard at the temples with my thumbs. "I've never experienced anything like this. A cursed doll that's wreaking havoc? I mean, how do you fight something like that?"

"You've got to get to the core of his existence," Patrick says.

"And how do I do that?"

"With Farah's help, like she said."

I shake my head and feel the tears coming again. "Farah was so talented and had such a promising future. I don't get how to justify the death of a person like that."

Patrick rubs my neck. "Everything happens for a reason."

I groan. "Everyone keeps telling me that. *What* is the reason, though?"

"I don't know, babe. I just don't." His eyes get all serious and he gazes at me thoughtfully. "What I do know is that with our combined talents and abilities, we can fix this. Remember everything that Oliver and the counselors taught us at the retreat. We have to research and explore and investigate and use our senses and deductive reasoning to get to the heart of this matter and then figure out how we're supposed to help." He takes a deep breath. "Kendall, not only do we have to help Farah pass, we have to help whatever or whoever is possessing Xander the Doll. We have to help the Farnsworth family. The pain is obviously deep and intense and it's been here too long."

Sitting up, I swivel on the swing to get a good look at the guy I've fallen so hard for. His kind eyes, his strong chin, chiseled nose, and firm lips. I move my hands over his cheeks and jaw and pull him toward me, needing to feel life flowing.

His kiss is soft and sweet, healing and therapeutic. I kiss him back with all the emotion I can muster up, relishing the feel of him underneath my fingertips.

"I'm crazy about you, Kendall," he says at last.

My heart pounds away like a ticking time bomb, ready to explode with my newfound love for him. "Ditto, Patrick. You've changed my life. You understand me. We're alike."

"We're meant to be," he says and then kisses me again.

I pull back moments later, but not in a bad way. This isn't the most opportune time to ask this, but I have to.

"Say . . . will you go to my prom with me? It's in a few weeks and hopefully we'll have all of this Xander crap solved and I'll have my DNA test results and you can be with the new Kendall Moorehead."

The corner of his mouth lifts. "I kinda like the current Kendall Moorehead."

"You know what I mean," I say, smiling.

Patrick picks up my right hand and kisses the top, then turns it over and presses a kiss to my palm. I'm going to melt here on the spot. "I'd be honored to come to the prom with you."

We make out a little while longer and then Patrick forces himself to leave.

"I've got to get home. School tomorrow, you know? But I'll be here Friday afternoon. You and Celia see what you can do to get us in that Farnsworth House for a *real* investigation. It's the key to everything, I just know it."

I throw myself onto him, hugging him with all my might. He hugs me back and plants one last kiss on me.

I wait until his car pulls out of the drive and disappears up the road. I need to collapse on my bed for the rest of the day. Yeah, yeah . . . I should work on that paper for Mr. Rorek, but there's still time. Up in my room, I remove Buckley and Eleanor from the pile of clothes on the floor and dig out my DKNY tank top and black shorts. I'm about to fling myself on the bed and curl up with the kitties when I realize I have unread e-mail on my computer screen.

"Oh God, please not the haunted-sandwich man." I walk over and scroll the mouse to see mail from none other than Taylor Tillson. It doesn't look like a forwarded joke; it seems more personal. I sit down in the chair and click to open the message.

My dearest Kendall!

*Bonjour* or *neenjit dôonch 'yáa,* as the native Alaskans say in their Gwich'in language. I'm sooooooooo sorry I've been so out of touch. I think of you, Celia, and Becca almost every day. Life is crazy here. Dad works all the time and I'm on my own a lot. I'm still into my photography and really need to set up a website for it. The beauty of the nature here is phenomenal. I actually got a picture of a bald eagle ripping a fish right out of the water. Oh, *mon dieu!*

I'm writing because Ryan called me and asked me to come back for the prom and go with him. Right . . . like I can afford a plane ticket all the way across the United States for a corsage, dinner, and a few dances? LOL! The real problem, though, is that I've fallen hard for a guy here. He's a little older than we are—okay, he's nineteen!—and *il est très magnifique!* He's working part-time with my dad at the park, but he's going to be backpacking in Europe all summer. I'm trying to get Dad to let me go with him. Who knows how that will turn out.

I've really fallen for Benjamin—that's his
name. And he is so into me. So I don't think it
would be appropriate for me to go to the prom
with Ryan. I sort of feel like I'm doing Ryan
wrong, but we had to break up, you know, when I
left Radisson. Same as you and Jason.

Speaking of which . . . he's an ass.

He hasn't e-mailed you, has he? He keeps asking
me if I've heard from you and I tell him to get
a life and contact you himself. I will tell
you—and I feel no loyalty to Mr. Overprotective—
but he hangs out regularly with this chick at
school. Her name is Zelda. Not even kidding you.
Who names their kid Zelda in this day and age?
I think her parents had a thing for F. Scott
Fitzgerald or something. But he and Zelda are
pretty much inseparable. I know you guys called
it quits; however, I'm still pissed at him for
not coming out and telling you about Zelda.
They go to the movies all the time, she drives
him home from school in her SUV—yes, she has an
Escalade, hello, gas guzzzzzzzler—and they are
just joined at the hip.

I didn't tell you that to hurt you, *mon amie*.
I see pics of a devilishly cute guy on your
Facebook page. Who's he? New boyfriend? I need
deets!

I hope you've moved on from Jason. I hope you're
not pining away for him, because, Kendall, he's

not worth it. He's my brother, my twin, and
I love him, but he's a guy. I don't want you
hurting over him. I want to know that you're
happy and doing your ghost-hunting thing—which
I miss almost as much as I miss you girls—and
taking care of Kendall.

I promise to be better about staying in touch.
As you know, it's hard fitting into a new place.
But Taylor Elizabeth Tillson is doing her best.
Don't you worry about me. *Je vais très bien.*

Write back when you can. And hey, if Dad will
let me do the backpack thing this summer, maybe
you can come along? Get out of Radisson? Let's
talk.

Love you like a sister!
Taylor ☺

I can totally hear Taylor's voice as I'm reading and rereading this e-mail. Glad to see that living in the frozen tundra hasn't changed her. And Jason? Well, I suppose that for him, change was inevitable. He moved on. I moved on. I'm in love with Patrick. And he's . . . well, he's hanging with *Zelda*. Funny, I always thought I'd be going to the RHS prom on Jason Tillson's arm. Now, my thoughts turn to dancing under the balloon ceiling and twinkling lights with Patrick Lynn. It's the next best thing to heaven.

First, though, I have to help Farah Lewis get to heaven and

her final resting place and put the legend of Xander the Doll to rest once and for all.

It seems like forever until Friday afternoon rolls around again. School isn't the same. How could it be when such a popular member of the campus royalty is no longer with us? A flier announcing Farah's opera recital still hangs on a locker in a tormenting reminder that her voice is silenced forever. Students wander around the halls laughing less and feeling a little bit numb. I can read the thoughts of so many people . . .

A freshman: *Why her?*

One of the motorcycle guys: *Did she have a seat belt on?*

A junior: *I heard she was speeding.*

The janitor: *Someone said she was on drugs. All of these kids are on drugs.*

A sophomore: *I can't believe that happened here in Radisson.*

A fellow student: *Farah and I were best friends in elementary school. I'm going to miss her so much.*

A teacher: *How do we talk to the kids about this?*

Time will heal the emotional wounds and shock at Radisson High. However, my ghost-huntress team is taking action to stop Xander the Doll from causing more chaos.

Patrick's back in Radisson. He drops his stuff off at Father Mass's and then comes over to my house. Celia, Becca, and Shelby-Nichole arrive and we all head over to the Radisson Historical Society as planned.

Mr. Pfeiffer opens the office door on the third buzzer ring. "Oh, it's you all again."

"Yes, sir," Celia says politely. "We'd like to talk to you about doing an investigation here."

He starts to close the door, but Becca puts her booted foot in the way. "Really, Mr. Pfeiffer. We've got too much weird shit going on in Radisson since Xander the Doll made his appearance at the county fair. I really think you should hear us out."

Sweat drips down his bald head, and he bites his bottom lip. Then he moves aside and grudgingly lets us in. We file past him into the great room, where we all sit on the antique furniture.

Louis Pfeiffer nervously moves about, twisting his hands together.

*This man knows a lot more than he's saying.*

*I'm sensing it too,* Patrick says to me.

"Please, Mr. Pfeiffer. Help us," I say, practically begging.

He lets out a long sigh. "You kids are going to cause nothing but trouble. I told the historical society board that we shouldn't have brought Xander out of the house. But no one listens to me. They thought it would get us some attention and bring in some donors to help us fix this place," he says.

Celia cocks her head. "I believe Mega-Mart gave a sizable donation to Farnsworth House."

"Yes, it did indeed. And that's the only reason I'm allowing you in here again," he notes.

Celia's ready to play hardball. "Mega-Mart is prepared to contribute more if you're willing to help us."

Wow . . . a little extortion in small-town America. Okay, whatever works. I can see the dollar signs spinning in Mr. Pfeiffer's eyes.

"Look, Mr. Pfeiffer. I'm not going to candy-coat this," I say. "Four people—all our friends—have had heinous things happen to them since meeting Xander the Doll and taking pictures of him. One even died."

"Oh, that young cheerleader," he says, shaking his head. "Such a sad story. Driving too fast like that. A tragedy and a waste."

"Yes, it was," I say. "One that could have been prevented had we known more about this curse that surrounds Xander the Doll."

His eyes shift around as if he's covering something up.

*He is covering something up,* Patrick says to me.

*I've never seen a person sweat like this.*

*He needs to pop a salt tablet . . . geesh!*

I stand and advance on the curator. "Mr. Pfeiffer, you said this place needs to be fixed. What did you mean by that?"

He hesitates for a moment. "The board doesn't want me talking about it."

"Why isn't this place open to the public?" Patrick asks.

"Again, that's the board's decision, not mine," the older man says.

Patrick slices his eyes over to me. *This is personal for him. Push him, Kendall. He'll break.*

"This doesn't make sense," I shout in frustration. "This has gone too far. I'm not trying to be disrespectful. There's something you're not telling us. A secret you're hiding that may cause more people to get hurt. Do you want that on your head, Mr. Pfeiffer? Do you want your children to know what you're doing?"

He lowers his eyes to the ground and begins pacing the room. "How do you know about my children?"

"I'm psychic, remember." Although I'm not picking up anything more specific, this may get him to talk. "Don't you want them to be proud of what you're doing here?"

His bottom lip quivers. "I don't know what to say. I'm just the caretaker. I have been for twelve years, since the board sought me out. I do what I'm told. I obey orders. I'm fifty-seven years old and I enjoy the steady paycheck from the board so my son can go to college at UGA and so I can have health insurance to cover my daughter's diabetes supplies."

"We're sorry about your daughter, Mr. Pfeiffer. Our friends the Lewises lost their daughter. Possibly because of Xander. Now, you know plenty about the history of this house and the family, and if you'll allow us to investigate and research, perhaps we can prevent another tragedy from occurring."

He drags his sleeve across his forehead to mop up the perspiration. "All right. I'll tell you what I know. The board is one person. It's the lone Farnsworth survivor. Her name is Abigail, and she's Robert Townsend Farnsworth's granddaughter. She lives in a nursing home in Macon and is very old and frail. Abigail made a deathbed promise to her father, Robert's son, that she'd always take care of Xander and he would always live in this house. However, when the economy crashed, a lot of the family's investments disappeared nearly overnight. The only way Abigail could keep the house was to donate it to the city as a tax shelter with the stipulations that the board control the day-to-day operations and that the city of Radisson wouldn't change anything about the building, disperse any of its contents, or open it to the public to judge. To get around the agreement and to raise some money, the historical society came up with the traveling exhibit, but Xander would return home to his room each and every night. That was, until weird things started happening, so we stopped the exhibit for a few years."

"Why bring him out now?"

"The county fair offered a nice donation for the exhibit and we couldn't turn it down."

Becca lowers the voice recorder that she's been using to capture the story. Celia cuts her eyes over to me; I sigh. "What do you think is going on here, Mr. Pfeiffer?"

"What do you believe is at play here?" Patrick asks.

The man holds up his hands. "I don't know. I don't want to know. I don't mess with anything and it doesn't mess with me." Fear resonates in his glassy eyes. More than fear. I sense a near panic from him. Dread is painted over his face from jowly cheek to jowly cheek, and for a moment, I believe he might cry. "Look, you're just kids. You don't have the responsibilities in life that I do. I do what I'm told; I collect my paycheck and go home every night. Xander, or *whatever*, leaves me be."

I swallow down my aggravation when I listen to the tremor in Mr. Pfeiffer's voice. Stepping forward, I put my hand gently on his arm. "We can help. If Xander is possessed by a spirit, we can help set it free and put it on its path to redemption and peace."

My fingers tingle with an unknown touch. My heart rate triples, and the psychic headache begins ticking away at me. Bits and pieces of time flash before me with vivid images that spark more curiosity than answers. A woman dancing around a fire. A boy crying in the blackness of his room. A whip striking skin, the color of it indiscernible. The fireworks of memories shift and I'm back in my dream . . . dark . . . dank . . . the tang of wet earth fills my nostrils. The shadows of many lost souls dancing around in confusion.

I jerk out of the image, and Patrick holds me to him. He felt it too. My senses tell me there's something very dark here. Darker than we've ever dealt with. It may be voodoo or black magic or just a spirit that's confused, hurt, and angry. But it must be revealed and cleansed.

"Help us," I plead in a whisper.

Mr. Pfeiffer's lip quivers. His voice drops to a whisper. "I-I-I can't get involved."

Celia puts her hands on her hips and nods to me.

I hold my head high. "Well, Mr. Pfeiffer, we *are* getting involved. Tomorrow night, we're bringing our equipment and we're doing an investigation."

He sees that I'm not messing around.

"I'll leave the key under the mat," he says finally. "There's one stipulation."

"Name it," Celia says.

"You can't reveal your findings to the public."

"Agreed," Becca says on our behalf.

This doll has an attachment, and it's pissed. This has to be solved immediately.

"We have to do this for everyone who's ever been hurt by Xander. We have to do this for Farah."

## Chapter Fifteen

AROUND NINE THIRTY SATURDAY MORNING, I stretch like one of my kitty cats and reach for my BlackBerry on the nightstand. The *bleep-bleep-bleep* of incoming text messages has woken me from a sound snooze. I smile when I read them:

> Morning baby

> Last nite wuz fun. Just the 2 of us. 2nite will b diff

Patrick and I had just curled up together on the couch at Father Mass's and watched *Casablanca*, which was exactly what we both needed to get our minds off the turmoil in town, to have some alone time, and to prepare for what we might face this evening. I run my thumbs over the small keypad to respond.

> Hi u! I no. Last nite wuz a blast.

> Worried @ 2nite

> Don't b. I've dealt w/worse

> u don't know that

> we never no what we're up against

> i'll b w/u the whole time

> going 2 ask Loreen and Mass 2 b there

> coming over?

> in a bit to Loreen's store

> i'll grab a shower & meet u there

> sounds good 2 me

> c u then

I let out a majorly contented sigh and then hop out of bed. After I take a quick shower, blow my hair into some semblance of a manageable style, and throw on jeans and a tank, I race through the kitchen—stopping long enough to fill the parentals in on where I'm off to—and then jump in the car and head over to Loreen's.

As I arrive, Loreen is standing outside the shop, locking the door.

"What's going on?" I ask.

"There you are, Kendall," she calls. "We're meeting Mass and Patrick down at the café for some breakfast."

The grumble at the bottom of my stomach tells me that it's most definitely interested in some food. "Sounds awesome."

We get to the Radisson Café, where I see Father Mass and Patrick already have a booth for us. Loreen slides in next to her boyfriend and I do the same with mine.

My eyes smile up at Patrick and he leans in for a kiss hello. In my peripherals, I see Loreen and Mass do the same thing. Momentarily, my psychic vision kicks in and I see Loreen and Mass together, kissing in a very public way, surrounded by people. I jump when the image leaves me as quickly as it came.

"Everything okay?" Patrick asks.

"Yeah, fine. Fine." I don't want to read anything into what I just saw, so I grab the small menu and drool over my meal of choice.

"I'd like the smoked Gouda, ham, and spinach omelet, please," I say to the waitress. Patrick orders the lox, onion, and cream cheese omelet, while Loreen and Mass agree to split the Healthy Platter, which is anything but—three scrambled eggs, bacon, sausage, three pancakes, and hash browns. "Do you need a defibrillator with that?"

Loreen tosses a creamer at me and we laugh. Then, like that, we turn our attention to more serious matters.

Patrick sips his coffee and then begins. "Thanks for meeting us, you guys. We've got a hell of a case we're dealing with tonight and we're going to need all the help we can get."

Father Mass speaks to me. "Patrick's filled me in on what's been going on over at the historical society and how you think this Xander the Doll has been causing trouble for a lot of people." He scratches at his night's growth of beard and continues. "I must say that I'm not altogether convinced that a doll is the reason for car accidents, house fires, and motorcycle crashes, but then again, Kendall, I've experienced a lot with your group, so I'll give you the benefit of the doubt."

"Me too," Loreen says. "Besides, I've heard the tale of this doll and the sad ending of the slave nanny who made him. I believe she was lynched. My senses are telling me that you need to focus your energies on her history."

"I have," I say. "Well, a little bit. She was rumored to be heavily involved in voodoo, and I'm just so afraid of even Googling information on that." Or my mother finding out that I was looking it up.

"It's okay to research, Kendall," Patrick says firmly. "Knowledge is power."

"Here y'all go," the waitress sings out as she balances our breakfast dishes up her left arm. She doles out the meals, refreshes the coffee, and leaves us to our conversation.

I dig into my smoked Gouda omelet like I've never seen food before, letting the steaming egg and cheese warm my insides.

"Father Mass?" I ask with my mouth impolitely full. "What do you know about voodoo? Do they, like, make you study other religions and stuff in seminary?"

He nods as he's sipping his coffee and then sets the cup down. "I've studied practically every known religion in the world."

"Tell us what you know."

Father Mass puts his elbows on the table. "From what you've told me, the slave woman, Althea, was from the West Indies, or as you know it today, Haiti. So more than likely, she practiced Haitian vodoun, which is based on the merging of the practices and beliefs of West African people's Arawakan religion and the practices of Roman Catholic Christianity. See, all of these African slaves were brought to Haiti in the sixteenth century along with their traditional beliefs. However, they were forced to convert to the religion of their owners."

"No freedom of religion back then," I quip.

He continues. "Vodouisants believe in one Supreme Being, called Bon-Dye, but they also worship several lesser spirits that they call the *loa*." He gestures with his hands. "They're actually quite spiritual in their belief and had to work in a lot of the elements from Catholicism in order to hide their religion from their owners. The Bon-Dye is unreachable, so they use the *loa* as their way to speak to their Supreme Being. Now, the *loa* are related to the African gods they left behind and may be spirits of natural phenomena—wind, fire, water—or of their dead ancestors."

"Yikes, it seems like a complicated religion." Me, I prefer the Father, Son, and Holy Spirit, the Book of Common Prayer, a little hymn singing, and a whole lot of faith and prayer. But to each his own. Who am I to say who's right and who's wrong?

"Where do things like voodoo dolls come into play?" Patrick asks. "I mean, is it possible that Xander the Doll is a voodoo doll that was charmed in some way by Althea?"

"Loreen and I have talked about this," Father Mass says. "In my studies, I've read that the *loa* have the power to make their presence known and can temporarily displace the astral body of a living person and occupy his or her physical body; effectively, a possession by the *loa*. Priests and priestesses preside over ceremonies of this nature."

Loreen takes over. "My theory is that Althea, a *manbo,* or priestess, conducted a ceremony of some sort that possessed Xander the Doll. That's why your friends who disrespected him have had bad things happen to them."

"I don't know about that, Loreen," Father Mass says. "It's not in my nature to believe in gods other than my own, but I do believe in evil entities out there."

"As do I," she says. She adds, "Vodoun, as Mass has explained, is a very devout religion. It's not the Satan worshiping portrayed in movies. A lot of the ceremonies are about protection of their family and loved ones."

"Xander the Doll hasn't been protecting anyone," I say through gritted teeth.

"That's just it," Loreen says. "He *may* be protecting someone and we just don't know it. There may be more to it than you know. If there's a way to connect with the spirit of this slave woman . . ."

"Do we know where she's buried?" Patrick asks.

I shake my head.

"I guess we start with the house, then," he tells me. "I wonder if we can get an up-close-and-personal interview with Xander. Maybe do some EVP work with him or let you try out your psychometry?"

"Do you actually think Mr. Pfeiffer will allow that?"

"He doesn't have to know," Loreen says. "I feel that the doll is a representation of a specific person. From what I know about people using voodoo dolls, you can address the doll almost as if you're talking to the person. You can ask for anything your heart desires because the doll calls upon the *loa* to fulfill your wishes or dreams."

"Is there any way to uncharm it?" I ask.

Patrick toys with his fork. "We'll do our best tonight."

I turn back to the adults. "You'll come with us, right? We don't know what we're up against and it's always good to have you two around."

I feel Father Mass's hesitation before he responds. "Well, Loreen and I sort of had . . . umm . . . personal plans for tonight."

She places her hand on his. "Aww, honey. It's just dinner. We can reschedule, can't we?"

A shadow of displeasure crosses my Episcopal priest's handsome face. "Well . . ."

Suddenly, I'm blinded by a flashing white light, warm and welcoming and emitting love. There's nothing bad, evil, demented, or frightening about it. It sparkles and shines and radiates pure happiness unlike anything I've ever experienced. It's . . . OMG!

Loreen is walking down a flower-strewn aisle dressed in white lace and tulle. Father Mass waits at the end of the path, his hand reaching toward her.

I jolt out of the trance, and my eyes fill with tears. I can't stop smiling at my mentors, people I brought together.

Her eyes shift over me, and then Loreen begins to cry as well. She's seeing exactly the same vision. There is no sadness on her face. Only pure joy at the realization of what we've both foreseen.

"What is wrong with you two?" Mass asks with great concern.

Patrick must have seen it too because he nudges me and says, "Shhhhhh . . . don't spoil it."

Father Mass looks at Loreen, me, Patrick, back to Loreen, and then he collapses in the booth with a long sigh of defeat. "You know, don't you?"

"Ummm . . . yeah," I say, beaming at the priest.

"You damn psychics ruin everything," he says with a smile in his voice.

Loreen launches herself into his arms. "Oh, Maaaaasssss!"

He holds her tightly and says close to her ear, "You can't even let me propose in the right way."

Patrick and I simultaneously reach for each other's hands as we watch the miracle unfold before us.

Loreen pushes back a little. "Does it really matter?"

"To me it does. Let me out."

Loreen moves out of the booth and Mass stands up. In the small café in downtown Radisson, mere steps from Divining Woman, my priest kneels down on one knee on the floor. He withdraws a small white box from the pocket of his jeans and presents it to her.

I gasp and squeeze Patrick's hand.

"Will you do me the great honor of marrying me, Loreen Woods?"

She opens the box and puts her hand to her heart. I don't know how she can focus on the glittering diamond nestled in the red velvet.

Mass actually seems nervous as he awaits her answer. "Well?"

Laughing through her tears, Loreen says, "Of course I will!"

*Phew!*

He slips the dazzling stone onto her finger and she slides off the bench and onto the floor with him, where they kiss in celebration. Patrick releases my hand and then hugs me to him, giving me a quick peck in honor of our friends.

"Okay, you two," I say kiddingly.

"Sorry," Loreen says, blushing.

"So, I guess this means you're ghost hunting with us after all?" Patrick asks with a laugh.

"All right, all right," Mass says.

They both get up and return to the table, gripping each other. I've never seen two people so happy, so in love, and so meant for each other.

At least *something* good is happening in this town.

# CHAPTER SIXTEEN

THAT NIGHT, OUR TEAM SHOWS UP at Farnsworth House. Great trepidation trills underneath my skin, but I tamp it down and force my feet toward the ancient building. No one other than Patrick seems particularly disturbed by tonight's investigation, but then again, they can't sense and feel what we can. Patrick is quiet as we walk in. I know he's concerned as well, though he's trying to hide it to keep me calm. Celia's got on her ghost-hunting vest and has every piece of equipment in her arsenal. She looks totally ridonkulous and adorable at the same time.

"What are those?" I ask as we unload everything from our cars before going inside.

"Oh, these are my new devices from Digitaldowsing.com." She holds up a small device with a couple of switches and a speaker on it. "This is a PX, which is an array of sensors that sample environmental data, sum the values into an integer, and associate that integer with a word from the device's dictionary." Another black box with a silver switch. "And this is the EM Pump. It creates a man-made magnetic field that's thought to be a catalyst for spirit manifestations."

I hold up my hand to keep her from going off the scientific deep end. "These are all great, Cel. I don't think I need to know more. Just tell me the results."

She smiles at me and tucks the tools back into her vest.

Shelby-Nichole is toting a digital camera, a video camera, and three infrared cameras to set up in the house. Becca's got her recorders and her computer with speakers and the software program Audacity to review any EVPs.

Me, I've got my pendulum, a bottle of holy water, my Grandma Ethel's cross, and a sensible pair of tennies on my feet.

"You ready for this?" Patrick asks. He spent the past two hours meditating in preparation for whatever we encounter tonight. He's about as relaxed as one can be, I would think.

"As ready as possible to delve into the unknown." I'm a bit uneasy, but I no longer fear the spirits, no matter how snarly they are. I dealt with my anxieties at Oliver Bates's retreat and I know that no matter what, God will protect me, especially since I'm doing what He wants me to do.

Father Mass and Loreen arrive, and we're ready to roll.

"You kids are in charge," he says. "But I'm here if you need me for anything."

We proceed up the walkway that cuts through the perfectly manicured lawn. The last remnants of the April sunset streak the sky in a fiery orange. By the time we've got the base camp set up, it'll be pitch-black outside. Just the right setting for a ghost hunt.

Mr. Pfeiffer scowls heavily as he lets us into the manor. "It's about damn time," he says gruffly. "My wife had to put dinner in the oven."

"We told you we'd be here after sunset," Celia says.

He lets out a harrumph and begins gathering his things. "You have access to the house, as promised. But leave everything exactly the way you found it."

"We promise," Celia says. She holds her hand out. "The keys, please?"

"Right, right." The man digs into his suit-coat pocket and produces a knot of silvery keys. "Leave them in the flowerpot on the porch when you're done tonight. Make sure you lock everything back up."

"We will, Mr. Pfeiffer," Celia says. Then she adds, "Thank you, sir."

I let out a sigh as I watch him disappear into the darkness. "Okay, let's get started."

With that, we disperse to wire the house with cameras and recorders. Celia sets up the computer monitor that allows us to see the IR cameras placed throughout the mansion. She and Becca walk around with the EMF detectors getting base readings on the property. Loreen, Patrick, and I go into the great room and take a seat on the couch to do some deep breathing. My palms are itchy, and my blood swooshes through my veins like raging river rapids. That nagging little psychic headache is starting to flare, letting me know that there will definitely be spirit activity here tonight.

I hear the floor creaking over my head, but it's just the team exploring up there. Shelby-Nichole and Father Mass were going to try to do some EVP sessions while Celia and Becca completed their walk-through. I'm just sitting here waiting for the spirits to start coming to me. Remarkably, the airwaves are silent for the time being.

Until . . .

"No way!" Becca stands to my left in front of the massive fireplace that dominates the room. "What the hell? Look at these EMF spikes I'm getting." She waves the device in front of the brick hearth and it lights up like the Las Vegas strip at midnight.

"There aren't any wires in there that could cause that," Celia the scientist says.

"Something's making it go apeshit," Becca says. "Kendall, are you sensing anything over in this area?"

I'm skeeved out in general by this whole house, but I can't pinpoint anything yet. "I don't know" is all I can respond.

Celia jots down the EMF-device information in her notebook. "I've made a note of it and we'll come back to it later."

She plops down on the antique marble coffee table and shows me her drawings of the floor plans. "So here's what we're looking at. Kitchen, downstairs bedrooms, which were more than likely the slave quarters, considering how small they are and how many of them there are. Upstairs is more bedrooms that would've housed the sixteen Farnsworth children. And right here—this must be Xander's suite," she says, pointing out a corner room on the second floor. She reaches for the keys. "Reckon one of these opens Xander's room?"

"Maybe so," I say. However, I'm not ready to see the doll yet. Not until we can connect with the spirits that might be—

*Whoa . . .*

It's as if a stiff lake-effect breeze blows straight through the room swirling up into the fireplace. The temperature around me drops at least thirty degrees. A chill walks up my back, and the hairs on my arms poke out under the goose bumps. A spirit is definitely here.

She appears right next to me. "It's about time y'all came over. Wait'll I show you the things I know about this place," the feminine voice says.

Farah Lewis still wears her red RHS cheerleader uniform, and she has her hands on her hips like she's about to start cheering. She walks right through Celia to take a seat opposite me. *Holy crap!* With everything going on, the fact that Farah is still earthbound slipped my mind. I haven't told anyone other than Patrick about her.

*Told me what?*

*Farah is here.*

*Where?*

*Over there.*

*You didn't tell anyone else you saw her before?*

*It was such a quick contact, and I hadn't heard from her since.*

*And she's here now?*

*Yeah . . . in the gold chair.*

*I don't see her.*

*Well, I do.*

"Are you okay, Farah?" I call out.

Celia jerks her head around. "Farah's here?"

Farah leans forward and tries to poke Celia in the back. "Yeah, Nichols! Right here. Behind you." Then the ghost glances at me. "She really can't see me?"

"No, she can't see you," I say.

"I can't see her," Celia says dejectedly.

"No way." Farah's beautiful white smile dazzles me. "You really *can* see spirits, Kendall. Courtney was wrong to treat you like she did. And I was wrong to go along with the queen beeyotch. Forgive me for that, will you?"

"No worries, Farah. It's all water under the bridge."

"Good, 'cause now that I'm on this plane, I'm all into happiness and light and doing the right thing. It's quite refreshing," she says with a dreamy smile.

Becca moves her digital voice recorder over and sets it in the empty gold chair.

Farah giggles. "Should that have tickled me?"

I grin. "Did it?"

"Sort of."

"So, what are you doing here, Farah?"

She moves her eyes around, getting a good look at the room. "I'm not really sure. After my funeral, I sort of wandered around town, and I ended up here. I guess I was seeking out that silly doll that I ticked off. He's upstairs in his case, you know. I had a long talk with him, and we've been setting things straight."

"What things?"

"You know, like I'm sorry I took his picture, didn't mean to disrespect him, blah, blah, blah." She stands and circles the area. "You have *no* idea the secrets this house has. More than anyone in this town could ever imagine."

"Why don't you tell me?" I ask.

Farah smiles and laughs again. "Now, you know that's not how it works, Kendall."

Just then, Shelby-Nichole and Father Mass come bounding down the stairs. "We got *the* most amazing class-A EVP," she says.

"I'll admit it's pretty impressive," Father Mass says.

Farah closes her eyes and waves her hand. "Go ahead. I wanna hear this too."

We all gather around and Shelby-Nichole presses the button on her recorder. I listen closely to the convo as it plays out:

> SHELBY-NICHOLE: Are there any spirits here with us? Okay, that was a dog barking outside.
> FATHER MASS: Are you suffering? May I pray for you?
> VOICE: *Yessss . . . please do.*

"Wow," Celia says. "That's clear. Female voice, definitely."

"Shhh!" Shelby-Nichole says. "There's more. Listen."

FATHER MASS: Do you know the nature of your
condition?
VOICE: *Deeeeeeecccccccceaaaasssssed.*

"Deceased?" Loreen asks.

"That's it," Becca notes. "I can clean that up later."

"Here it comes," Shelby-Nichole states.

FATHER MASS: Do you know why we're here?
Do you have a message for us?
VOICE: *. . . go down . . . underground.*

We all jump back. "Whoa!" is the collective opinion of the
group.

"That was amazing," Celia says.

"Unbelievable," Patrick adds. "One of the best EVPs I've
heard."

Farah is right next to me. "Yep. That's her. The lady I've
been hanging with."

"Her?" I ask the ghost.

"Yeah, she's really nice. We bonded about how my grandparents are from Ghana. She was originally from Ghana, but
then she was put on an African slave ship and sent to the West
Indies."

I don't need to be psychic to figure this out. "Are you talking about Althea, the Farnsworth children's nanny?"

Smiling, Farah says, "I think that's what she said her name was."

Turning to my friends, I ask, "What does the voice—Althea or whoever—mean by 'go down . . . underground'?"

"Underground Atlanta?" Shelby-Nichole asks, unaware of my conversation with the recently deceased.

Celia scoffs. "No, that's not it."

"Maybe it has something to do with the Underground Railroad?" Loreen suggests.

"There's no proof or history that it ran through Radisson," Celia the history buff says.

Farah tries to nudge me, but of course, nothing happens. "That's not necessarily true."

I spin on my heels. "The Underground Railroad came through this house?"

Becca turns around. "*Who* are you talking to?"

Celia answers, "She's connected with a spirit in the house."

I bite my bottom lip.

"Go ahead, Kendall," Patrick encourages me. "Tell her."

I breathe in deeply. "Farah Lewis is standing right next to me."

Becca's eyes grow wide. "She is? Seriously?"

"Hi, Rebecca," Farah says, although my friend can't hear her.

"She says hi to you," I say. Patrick nods at me, urging me to come clean to everyone. "Farah was at her funeral and spoke to me. She said it was Xander that caused her accident. She's been wandering the town and ended up here. It seems she has befriended . . . Althea."

"The nanny slave that made Xander?" Celia asks.

"One and the same."

"Wow," Becca says. "That means her spirit hasn't been at rest for more than a hundred and fifty years."

Snapping her fingers in perfect cheerleader style, Farah orders, "Oh, don't forget that part about this house having secrets."

I roll my eyes and repeat what she said.

"All houses have secrets," Celia quips.

"Not like this one," Farah says, and I relay her message.

Loreen steps forward. "Whatever this secret is hinges on the message we just got. 'Go down' and 'underground.'"

I turn my palms up and close my eyes. Stretching out with my energy, I try to connect with anything in the room that will talk to me, besides Farah. For a girl who died in such a horrific manner, her spirit is playful and silly. She stands in front of me making faces as I'm trying to do my psychic job. I wave her away and hang my head down, letting my hair cover my face in a veil of concentration. Remnants of my dream come back to me . . . the mustiness of the earth and the damp crawlspace . . . and maybe even something dangerous.

"There's something hidden underground here," I say with great confidence.

"Attagirl," Farah says, cheering me on and doing a bit of a routine I remember from basketball season. Why she can't just *tell* me, I don't understand.

Patrick steps in front of me. Quiet for the most part up until now, he reaches for my hand and tugs me over to the fireplace. "Becca picked up almost twenty milligauss in this area." We both begin feeling around the crevices and cracks in the mantel. Patrick sweeps his hand over and around the antique oil painting of a country landscape.

"Warmer," Farah says playfully.

I move to the right side of the fireplace and trail my hand down the wooden carvings around the perimeter of the pit. Knobs of whittled round wood knot the four corners in a decorative pattern that doesn't match the rest of the house's architecture. My fingers brush around the smoothness and a message comes to me—from deep in the recesses of my mind—that these are for more than decoration.

"You're getting warmer," Farah says again.

Patrick cocks his head at me. "There's some sort of passage here, Kendall."

"I know."

"Push the knob in, if you can," he instructs.

With a grunt and a groan, I shove hard into the structure. "It won't budge," I say with a moan.

"Ahh, you're red-hot!" Farah says, clapping. "Go, Kendall, go, Kendall . . ."

"Farah, please! You're not helping."

She stops and pouts a bit and then returns to her dance routine.

I do a good heave-ho, and the knobs pop back into the wood like something out of an Indiana Jones movie. I half expect a gigantic boulder to roll down from somewhere and crush me. Thankfully that's not the case. Patrick triumphs on his side of the mantel, as well.

"Holy crap! I can't friggin' believe it!" Becca exclaims.

The house groans and the floor begins to shudder underneath us. The wood panels of the mantel begin receding into the bricks, and the bottom of the fireplace shifts backwards, the plate slipping into the wall.

"It's some sort of secret passageway," Celia shouts. "It's the message: go down . . . underground. Do you think this was part of the Underground Railroad?"

"I haven't a clue," I say, exhausted after opening this channel.

Celia moves in front of me and starts to cough from the dust and cobwebs. "Oh my God—there's a staircase!"

"Awesome!" Becca shouts. "Can we fit down there?"

"We may be a little tall," Patrick notes. "We'll make it work, though. Celia, do you have flashlights?"

"Is the pope Catholic?" She pulls out her large LED lantern and splits it into three, handing one piece each to Patrick and me.

"I don't know, kids," Father Mass interrupts. "If there's a tunnel under there, it's probably as old as the house. You don't know how stable it is. Or how *unstable* it is. Something could happen down there and you could be trapped."

"That's why you and Loreen should stay here in case we need you to get help," Celia instructs.

I'm too dumbfounded at what's going on. Not only is there a secret passageway in here, but it exactly matches the vision from my dream. It's like I was led here. And I have no choice but to see this through.

Patrick looks over at me and quotes the EVP. "'Go down.'"

Giving a weak smile, I say, "What are we waiting for?"

## CHAPTER SEVENTEEN

THE STAIRCASE IS RICKETY and creaks as it guides us down, down, down into the earth below this house. I can't believe I'm putting my trust in some architect or carpenter from over a hundred years ago. Will this structure support the weight of all of us, or will we plummet into some never-ending hole?

I point the flashlight in front of me so I won't trip and fall and break my neck. Timidly, I place my sneakered foot on the wooden slat and proceed downward. So far, so good. Patrick is in the lead and he hasn't fallen in yet, so I'll up the faith ante. Celia's next, with Shelby-Nichole snapping pictures in our wake. Becca—brave Becca—pulls up the rear.

I sneeze, once—twice—a third time, feeling the chill of the darkness around me.

"Bless you," Celia calls.

"Are you all right?" Patrick asks, and I nod in the shadow of the flashlight.

"As all right as I can be considering the circumstances."

At the base of the stairs, a path spreads out in front of us. It's narrow and doesn't provide much headroom at all. We all have to duck to get under the low ceiling, especially Celia and Patrick. Dirt clods fall from the ceiling onto my skin and clothing as we pass, perhaps disrupted for the first time in a century and a half.

"How did someone dig this tunnel?" Becca asks.

"There's no telling," Shelby-Nichole answers. "Seriously, this looks like something that could help slaves escape. Why else would it be here?"

"And right under the master's nose in his great room. That's ballsy," Becca adds.

I want to agree, although I sense there are too many spirits trapped down here for me to believe they all actually made it out to see their freedom. The cries of people from a long-past era still linger. Not just men and women fighting for a way out, but children . . . babies. The agony of so many makes me want to double over in pain. My nostrils are filled with the stench of body odor and rotten food. I gag and try hard not to get sick right here, right now. It's not real. It's place-memory I'm picking up with my psychic sensors. *Breathe . . . just breathe . . .* Nameless, faceless souls circle the very air around me, extending their tortured fingers toward me for help.

"Patrick," I moan, tortured by what I'm seeing.

"I know, Kendall. I'm getting it too." Patrick turns back for my hand and immediately shares my vision. "We can't help them all."

"Why not?"

His eyes are black in the tunnel. "We'll try."

I take a sip of water he offers me from the bottle he pulls from his back pocket. Quenching my own thirst seems to disperse the spirits loitering here. I so much want to cleanse the whole area and help them all pass on to their own personal paradises. If I even can.

"I'm freezing," Becca exclaims as we press forward through the crumbling passageway.

Celia jeers. "We are, like, underground. There will be a marked temperature difference from the surface."

"It's more than that," I say, agreeing with Becca. "We're surrounded by phenomena. These spirits are confused. Some are hurt. Most are baffled over their state of being, thinking that their slave lives still exist." Their jumbled whispers join together in an off-key opera, crying out to anyone who can hear them for help.

I press my hands up to my ears, hoping to drown out their sorrow, but it continues to echo against my eardrums. I can't see any of them, yet their heartache is so intense, fiery, and *real* to me. "Farah, can you help me?" I ask. I see my breath in the light of the flashlight, as if it's a January afternoon in Chicago.

"Come on, Kendall," she says sweetly. "You're doing great so far." She curls her index finger, and I move ahead of Patrick to follow the specter.

My shoe hits a puddle on the floor, splashing mud up onto my jeans. Dirt scatters from overhead, and I try not to dwell on being buried alive as an avalanche of small pebbles pound my skull. I duck and cover my head as Patrick calls out to me. Surely this isn't the way things end for us, particularly when we're trying to help those in need.

"It's okay. It's settled now," Patrick says.

I stand as tall as I can and forge ahead. I can't let anything stop me. I have to see this through. Around the next turn, I run face-first into a damn-near-primeval cobweb. It's the one from my dream trying to ensnarl me. The wispy threads layer over my face, and I start sputtering, coughing, and flailing my hands around to rid myself of the insect's prison. I run forward, fearful that the owner of the web is now in my clothing. For a moment, I almost whip my T-shirt over my head to remove the pesky, multilegged creatures. Man, it must have had babies and they're crawling all over me. I wipe my hands up and down my arm to get off the bugs. I won't let them defeat me. I won't be scared. I won't give in! Then I realize it's not bugs at all. I'm only feeling the emotions and experiences of what those escaping slaves went through.

"Keep up, Kendall," Farah calls out. "We're almost there. You're not going to believe it."

"Patrick, stay with me," I yell out.

"I'm right behind you, babe," Patrick says through the darkness. "Wait up."

I stop in the tunnel, hunching down so the dirt ceiling won't shower me with more clods and God knows what else that has gathered down here all these years. I will my pulse to calm the hell down and I try to breathe through my panic. It's just spiders and other bugs. I've handled worse. At least, I think I have.

Then a bloodcurdling scream twists through the air.

"Gross! Gross! Gross!" Shelby-Nichole dances around spastically, pressing herself up against the dirt wall as hard as she can. "It's a snake!"

Becca shines her light at Shelby-Nichole's feet to show the skin of a snake.

"It's just the skin it shed," Celia says.

"I don't care! It's a damn snake. I don't like this at all," Shelby-Nichole calls out. She begins to cry and tremble at the same time. "I-I-I thought I could be all brave like y'all and do this—I can't though. I frickin' hate spiders and I loathe snakes. I can barely breathe in this claustrophobic space." She backs up into Becca, and all I want to do is calm the freak-out before it gets out of control. "I'm scared shitless and I want out. Please don't hate me."

"We don't hate you, Shelby-Nichole," I say. "Just head back the way we came and stay by the mouth of the staircase. You don't have to do anything you don't want to."

A sigh of relief escapes her chest and I watch as she swats away the tears on her cheeks. "I'm sorry, y'all."

I'm sort of jealous that she can admit her weakness so boldly and back out. I can't though. I have to keep going.

"Don't be sorry," Celia says, and I know that she's not altogether brave in this environment, but we all press forward. It's now just Patrick, Celia, Becca, and me . . . and, of course, Farah leading the way.

"We're so close. Just watch out for the big holes in the floor," she instructs.

Too late. I have no time to pass on the warning to Patrick, who trips and goes sprawling on the floor, landing with a resounding groan. Mud splashes and he's covered in red Georgia clay all over the front of him. "I'm okay."

"Oh, sweetie," I say, trying to brush the mud off.

"It's okay, Kendall," he says and winks at me. "In fact, I'm glad that happened. I'm connecting with the soil. It's . . . speaking to me."

"What's it saying?" Becca asks.

"Mainly to keep going."

Farah throws her hands up. "Umm, duh! That's what I've been saying, cute boy."

I shine the beam up ahead, seeing that the tunnel gets smaller and smaller until it's only a crawlspace. Are you kidding me? I sigh extra-hard, then get hold of myself. Okay, if that's what it takes. I get on all fours, move my hair aside, and crawl through the moist and musty dirt, trying not to sneeze. I hope there's a payoff at the end of this tunnel—freedom, a secret chamber, anything.

I'm not disappointed when I emerge from the tunnel into a small room at the end of the hall.

I gasp in the dull, clammy air, feeling suffocated almost. The space before me is not much bigger than my closet at home;

enough room to walk around, but you wouldn't want to be stuck in here for any length of time. Stacked up in one corner are rusted buckets from an era long past. A wobbly old wooden chair is propped against another wall, and I see a moth-eaten, filthy blanket covering what seems to be sticks.

I move toward it and reach for a corner of the tattered fabric.

"Kendall, don't!" Patrick shouts at me.

Too late. I scream out in terror at what I see. The slack broken jaw. The hollow eye sockets. The skull bashed in and the rest of the skeleton disintegrating here in this nearly airtight cell. Spiders, crickets, and other bugs I don't care to catalog scatter away from their hiding places, seeking shelter in other areas of the room, the cave, and the tunnel.

"Nasty!" Celia says when she enters the room.

I dive onto Patrick's chest—not caring that he's icky with mud—and he absorbs me into his embrace. My body shakes, not so much from the shock of finding the remains but because I know what happened to the man. He was tortured and . . . murdered.

"Told you this place is messed up, didn't I?" Farah says with a grin. "That poor guy. His is a sad tale. Can you believe that this house was a stop on the Underground Railroad?" She points at the end of the room where the tunnel continues on. "It goes another mile and comes out in the vacant field next to where they're working on Celia's dad's distribution center."

I pass the information to the rest of the group. Patrick begins to feel the clay walls with his hands. His eyes close, his lashes fluttering against his cheeks. I watch his chest rise and fall as he experiences his vision.

"There's a lot of pain and suffering here," he says, which appears pretty obvious. He continues. "People starved here. They had illnesses that prevented them from moving fast enough and . . . something happened as they were trying to make it out of the South."

He's right. A few made it, but there's an overwhelming cry of grief from the many, many, many who didn't get out.

"Let's keep going," I say, not even waiting for the others before I get back on all fours and crawl out the other end of the room.

Farah leads the way. I can barely keep up with her as I creep through the darkened cavity that carries us deeper and deeper. An overpowering sense of sadness washes over me as I think of all of those poor men, women, and children who attempted to gain their freedom this way. I marvel at the hours of work and toil crafting this duct to independence.

"There were a lot that got out, Kendall," Farah says. "I have to show you what happened, though."

We continue farther into the subterranean channel; Patrick, Celia, and Becca are on my flank. Our flashlights provide the only information about what we're getting into. My hope is we'll come out the other end free from encounters or danger, but I don't think this is how it's going to happen.

Farah disappears and I blink wicked hard to see up ahead.

The darkness is so black that my eyes are playing tricks on me—or are they? Shadows dance in the dimness, letting me know we're not alone. Silhouettes of long dresses and work clothes from another time march across the dirt floor, as if they're on the lookout for someone who might return them to slavery.

"We're not here to hurt you," I say to the outlines. "We just want to help."

They don't respond and only hunker away in apprehension.

It's at this point that I run into them. No, not the shadow people. The bars. Metal bars that have been screwed into the clay walls and bolted in securely. I stop, sit on my haunches, and spin the LED light around. I'm in another room, a bit larger than the previous one. But the bars stretch across like in a jail cell, halving the space. Beyond the bars, on the other side, the walls and ceiling have completely caved in. Red dirt is piled in uneven mounds, preventing any further exploration or escape.

"Why does this look like a prison?" I ask.

"Why not just seal up the tunnel?" Celia asks.

"That's the real question," Patrick says.

Farah materializes behind the bars, gripping them like she's a prisoner. "This is what you had to see, Kendall. Do you get it now?"

I address her with concern. "Someone purposely put this up to stop the slaves from leaving."

She bobs her head up and down. "Althea will tell you everything if you ask nicely."

# Chapter Eighteen

One of the shadow figures shifts, takes shape, and emerges from the dark.

There she stands, as real as I am.

"Can you see her?" I whisper to Patrick.

When his hand grips mine, I have my answer.

In the huff of a breath, the storied slave woman, nanny to Robert Townsend Farnsworth, and creator of Xander the Doll, appears right before us.

"Althea?"

The wrinkles around her eyes and mouth indicate how aged she was when she died. A streak of white hair extends from her right temple all the way back through her short jet-black hair. Her dress is drab and tattered, and she's wearing an apron that has seen much better days. Her eyes are the deepest black, and her face is tired, worn, and very, very bitter.

"Althea?" I repeat.

"What'chall doin' here?" she asks in a molasses Southern accent tinged with her African and West Indies heritage. "Don't y'all know this ain't no place to be? Ain't safe for neither man nor beast."

Approaching cautiously, I say, "My name is Kendall, Althea. My friend Farah brought me here to meet you."

Farah literally walks through the bars and sidles up to the slave woman. "These are my friends that I was telling you about. They can actually *see* us. They're the ones who can help."

The older woman lowers her gloomy eyes. "Ain't no one gonna help me. I couldn't protect those children, so who's gonna help an old woman like me?"

Patrick eases forward. "I'm Patrick, Althea. We've heard that you were the caretaker for the Farnsworth children. Is that what you mean? Are those the children you were protecting?"

Althea crosses the room and picks at a stain on her dress. Her hands work across the fabric just as if she were truly alive and animated with her love and care of the family in her keep. There's a deep sorrow, though, indicated by the worry lines in her forehead. The pain radiates off her in sheets of energy that fills the room.

"You made a doll for Robert Farnsworth. Do you remember?" I ask.

"Of course I do, missy. That doll was the world to that child."

Patrick asks, "Would you like to see him? Xander, that is."

Althea's wrinkles lift for a moment, but it's unclear what her answer is.

"Celia, go get it!" I say.

Without hesitation, my ghost-huntress partner drops to her hands and knees, and she heads back out the tunnel. I'm sure Mr. Pfeiffer isn't going to be happy at all that we're disturbing Xander, but my gut instinct tells me that the prized museum piece has got to be involved if we're to pass these ghosts on to their final rest.

"I'll go with her," Becca says. "You know, so she's not alone."

I mouth my thanks and turn back to the two spirits before me.

"What happened in here?" I ask, indicating the bars.

"Master found out 'bout the tunnel," Althea states. "Instead a destroyin' it straightaway, he made it a torture chamber. Dozens of my fella slaves was caught when them bars was put up. Most done died a no air or no food or just goin' plumb crazy."

"That's horrible and inhuman," Patrick says.

Althea nods her head.

Farah adds her two cents. "Merciless. Heartless. Brutal. Mean. Cruel. It all applies to him, according to Althea."

"I can't believe Phillip Farnsworth was so bastardly that he would let men, women, and children die of suffocation like this," I say, shaking my head in denial.

Anger highlights Althea's features and her nostrils flare. "Phillip Farnsworth was the devil in fine gentleman's clothin', I tell ya."

Farah elbows the slave woman. "Yeah, yeah . . . they've got to hear all that crazy family stuff you've been telling me. It's okay. Kendall and Patrick are cool."

I imagine that this woman has very little reason to trust me, considering my skin color matches that of the people who enslaved and murdered her. "You can tell me, Althea. I'm special. So is Patrick. We can see spirits like you and Farah. Folks who have passed on to another realm. If you'd like, we can help you find the light. All you have to do is ask for it."

"Chile . . . I done seen that light ya talk of. I gotta protect those in my care."

"Most of the Farnsworths have died," Patrick tells her. "Even Robert."

Althea looks as if she's going to cry. "I did everything to protect that boy."

Celia and Becca emerge from the tunnel with Xander the Doll. Loreen is behind them, dirty from head to toe.

"I had a sense that you needed me," she whispers, and she squeezes my arm.

"Thanks, Loreen."

"Look what we've got," Celia says in the general direction of Althea.

The woman's eyes shift to the doll. She makes as if to take him, but of course, she's not able. Celia cradles him in her arms while Althea stands next to her, gazing at Xander with trouble in her expression. She steps back and begins muttering a prayer under her breath.

"What is it, Althea?"

Her eyes open wide, heavy with despair. "Dat ain't da

Xander I made for muh boy. This doll's got the ol' man's evilness in him. I saw ta dat."

"I don't understand, Althea."

Tears well in her eyes. "I made Xander to protect Robert. I done put a blessin' in him ta keep muh Robert from harm. The *loa* went in Xander to watch muh boy and keep him safe."

Patrick furrows his brow. "Safe from who?"

"The devil himself!"

With that, Althea fades away.

I throw my hands up.

"What? What happened?" Becca asks. "What did she do?"

"She left," I say.

Farah shifts between Patrick and me. "Y'all, I've got to tell you more. Althea didn't lay down the whole narrative."

I instruct Becca to move the recorders in front of where Farah is standing. Celia's manning the video camera since Shelby-Nichole couldn't come down here. Loreen paces around the area where Althea had been as Patrick and I listen to the rest of the story. "Tell us, Farah."

Looking at her manicure, Farah begins the heartbreaking tale. "Not only was Daddy Farnsworth a real jerk to his slaves, he beat them and killed several of them with his horrible treatment. Including poor Althea. He also beat his children."

My mouth drops open.

"What?" Celia says, irritated that she can't hear this.

I fill her in, and Farah goes on. "When I say he beat them,

I mean horrible abuses, like locking them in closets and not letting them eat if they disobeyed him. A lot of mental shit too, like telling them they'd never amount to anything and beating their hands when they did something wrong in his eyes."

I gulp down the disgust in my throat at Farah's words.

"Althea was a house worker, so she helped some of the field hands get into the manor after dark while the master slept, to create what you see here. A lot of times she gave him a special concoction of roots and herbs that put him to sleep so he wouldn't hear anything. Took them three years of working every night until sunup. Once it was completed, Althea sent the others to freedom while she stayed behind."

At that moment, Althea returns, moving slowly around the room and taking over the story where Farah left off. "I hadda protect them Farnsworth children. Which I did the best I could. The *loa* went into the doll. Nuthin' but love for muh lil' Robert." Her facial expressions shift into a passionate hatred. "What'd it get me? Murdered, I tell ya. Accused of witchcraft and voodoo and hung from dat front tree out yonder by the master himself."

My hand flies to my heart. *That's* who lynched Althea? A well-respected citizen of Radisson, known to be a family man, had murdered his children's nanny. My heart feels as if it's died just a little bit as I listen to the stories of this totally barbaric time when one person could own another and do to that person whatever he saw fit. Monstrous. And not so long ago in our nation's history.

I need one particular question answered. "Why does Xander hurt people now? If he was created out of love to protect Robert, why has he been the catalyst of so much mischief and mayhem? So much that he has to be locked up in a museum."

A deep guttural groan escapes Althea and she hangs her head. Farah comforts her. "Go ahead, girlfriend. Tell them. It's why they're here." Silence, and then Farah says, "It's not *her* Xander that did all of that."

"This isn't the doll you originally made?" I question.

"Dat be the physical doll, but I done sum'thin' to it b'fore muh spirit left muh body."

I spread my hands wide, urging the woman to go ahead.

"I cursed the devil, I did. Master's soul done passed into the doll upon his death. Doomed to spend eternity dat way. For the misery and sorrah he caused ta so many."

Patrick scratches his head. "Let me get this straight. The soul of Phillip Farnsworth is in this doll. The protective charm you put on it for Robert was lifted at some point, and now this bitter man is stuck inside the toy."

Farah jumps back into the convo. "Decades and decades and decades, the man's been trapped in there. Isn't that justice? I mean, he believed all this weird shit and he beat people and it's only right that he suffer some. But like Althea told me, it seemed that over time, Phillip Farnsworth lashed out in the only way he could, and that was by getting revenge on people who disrespected him when they saw the exhibit. You know, like me."

"All you did was take a picture," I say.

"Yeah, but I wasn't supposed to. Farnsworth believed that if you took a picture of someone, it stole part of his soul," Farah explains. "Apparently, he's been enjoying his reign of terror and is continuing to inflict pain on others, like he did when he was alive."

I stave off the tears. "You shouldn't have died, Farah. You were so young, beautiful, and talented. You totally had a career in opera ahead of you."

She waves me off. "It was my time. I did disrespect the history, and Farnsworth scared the crap out of me when I was driving. But I had work to do here, you know? I had to bring you to Althea so you could make it all right. And do whatever ghostly investigative stuff you do to exorcise the wickedness inside the doll."

"That's a tall order," I say, wondering if I'm truly up to the task.

"We can do it, Kendall," Patrick says softly. "For Farah."

"What is she saying?" Celia asks, and I fill her and Becca in on the deets.

Becca harrumphs. "That's why the damn doll creeps me out so much."

"It's why it creeps everyone out," Celia corrects.

"Da man had to pay for his crimes to all da people, slave an' family alike," Althea says with such passion. "But now he had da power. I try ta stop him, but he too powerful. Massah's stronga than da *lou* dat went into the doll. I no leave dis place fer fear of what'll happ'n."

Loreen has been listening quietly but now she speaks up. "Althea, dear, my name is Loreen and I can see and hear you just like Kendall and Patrick. This story saddens me so because this attachment to your former master and the doll you lovingly made has kept your soul here, earthbound and enslaved by this man. We have to set all of you free. You, Farah, Farnsworth. You should pass into the light and be with your friends and family. Not be stuck here in . . . this place."

Celia shakes her head and repeats what Patrick said earlier. "So, Phillip Farnsworth's soul is in this doll and he's the one that causes all the trouble anytime people see the exhibit and don't, what—treat him like the fine Southern master that he used to be?" She turns the doll in her arms and looks Xander right in the button eyes. "You're an ass! You need to get over it, dude!"

As soon as the words leave her mouth, the ground rumbles something fierce, and a sinkhole opens up right underneath Celia. A shriek tears from her throat as she loses her balance and Xander spills onto the floor. He lands on his two feet, and the smile on his cloth face isn't so much a smile but a smirk of pleasure. Celia's gangly arms and legs fly up in the air and she trips, staggers, and falls into the three-foot-wide fissure.

"Celia!" I yell.

"Help!"

Patrick dives to grab her hand as she hangs on to the pit's edge and struggles not to plummet in. "Hold on to me, Celia!"

Becca stoops to grab Celia's waist, and I get her other arm. "I've got you too."

Farah's in the background doing one of the RHS cheers about "hold that line" as we strive to save Celia.

"There's nothing under my feet," she calls out, dirt covering her black hair. "Something's pulling me."

"Quick," Becca says.

Loreen holds Becca and then she, Patrick, and I do a massive jerk to yank Celia out of this situation. It's like we're fighting something though, and I toss a defiant stare over my shoulder at that damned (literally!) doll.

"Oh, we'll take care of you in a minute for doing this to my friend."

"Go, Kendall; go, Patrick; go, Becca," Farah cheers.

One last humongoid tug by all of us, and Celia is up out of the gap, righted, and standing on terra firma again. Exasperated, Celia brushes the dirt off of her clothing. "That was *not* cool." Then she grabs the doll and glares at him. "Your ass is grass and I'm the lawn mower. I don't care if you are historical."

I place myself between Celia and Xander the Doll, wrenching him from her arms. "We have to do this a certain way. Calm down, Cel."

Her eyes enlarge. "Did you *not* just see what happened? That thing is evil. *E. V. I. L.*"

"I agree. And we're going to take care of it." I release her and put down the doll, then shove my hands into my hair and massage my skull as I try to figure out the best way to bring this sitch to a positive close. I'm not exactly sure how to handle it. There are three souls at unrest that need to move on. I let out a long sigh and feel the irritation of it all sting me. I glance at Loreen for guidance. "What do we have to do to fix all of this?"

With no hesitation, she says, "We need to do a spiritual release."

"I don't know how to do that," I say.

Loreen takes my hand. "We'll do it together."

## Chapter Nineteen

Loreen tugs her bag of mystical items out of the tunnel behind her and begins to set up for the spiritual release.

"Do we need Father Mass?" I ask.

"No," Loreen assures me. "We'll be okay."

As Loreen is setting up candles, stones, and crystals on the floor, I turn to Althea. "Tell me more about the Underground Railroad."

"It be cuttin' right unda da massah's house and property."

"How many slaves were able to escape this way?" Celia asks.

"Oh, two or t'ree dozen."

"At least something good came out of this tunnel," Patrick says. "Althea, I'm sorry you had to suffer the way you did after all you did for the children of the family."

She smiles and lowers her eyes.

Farah bounds up to me. "So what are we going to do now?" She's so excited, like an overactive puppy at my feet.

"We're going to do our damnedest to get the spirit of Phillip Farnsworth to leave that doll."

She claps her hands. "Oh, goody! Then Althea and I can go, right?"

I feel a faint smile lift my lips. "That's all I want for you, Farah."

Loreen lights the end of her smudge stick and begins waving the putrid-smelling burned sage around the room. "There's too much pain, negativity, and suffering here."

Celia waves off the wisps of smoke. "We're all going to die from asphyxiation."

"Shhhh!"

We all circle together and sit, per Loreen's instructions. Patrick to my left; Celia to my right. We hold hands, close our eyes, and say the Lord's Prayer for protection. When I open my eyes, I see Farah and Althea standing behind our circle, watching.

Xander the Doll, or rather the physical home of the soul of Phillip Farnsworth, sits in the middle of the circle. "He looks so innocent. Yet he has done nothing but cause pain for people."

"Just like when he was alive; Phillip Farnsworth was a real sadist," Patrick notes.

"Let's all concentrate on the doll," Loreen instructs. "We're here to deal with the issues of grief and loss in this space, of the wounds inflicted upon the slaves and the children of the Farnsworth house and the trauma they may have carried throughout their lives. So unhealthy for anyone in that situation. Such negative energy built up, causing stress, fatigue, chakra block-age, even confusion and emotional and physical pain. We call upon the angels to guide us in our work here to free the trapped souls and lead them to a higher plane."

The energy in the room shifts. Not exactly sure how to de-scribe it, other than it's thick and heavy and hangs above me like it wants to drop and smash me. I protect myself in God's holy light, surrounding myself and my friends in a white bub-ble that nothing can penetrate.

"Come out of this doll, Phillip Farnsworth," Loreen says firmly, her voice deep and commanding. "Show yourself to us."

"The temperature just dropped twenty degrees," Celia notes, her thermometer in front of her. Her EMF detector is flashing vibrant red, indicating a strong energy.

"Phillip Farnsworth. You have a lot to answer for," Loreen says. "You have a lot of negative emotions that you need to own up to."

My throat constricts and I find it hard to swallow. The nor-mal *tap-tap-tap* of my psychic headache is more like a jackham-mer pounding into cement. I wince at the throbbing that also causes my eyes to twitch out of control. "You have a lot to an-swer for," I say, wondering where the words are coming from. "You've lived a life and afterlife of anger, shame, hurt, judgment, sadness, pain, and torture. You're a bad person, Mr. Farnsworth."

Celia and Becca gasp together and I jump. Xander the Doll falls over onto his side in the middle of the circle.

"He hears us," Loreen notes. "Phillip Farnsworth, we are

here to release your spirit from this doll. You have free will to leave it and pass on to the light, where you belong. There, you will be surrounded by your loved ones and those who passed before you. All you have to do is call out to them."

Patrick speaks. "We also send you our energy to cleanse this area, this house, and all those who've passed through this tunnel to freedom. We pray for the spirits that are trapped here and hope you'll find your peace too."

"Amen," Celia says.

I frown at her. "Not yet."

The iciness in the room increases, and we can all see our breath in front of us. Chill bumps cover my arms and my legs underneath my jeans.

Celia's teeth start chattering. "It's ridiculously cold in here."

"Something is definitely happening," Loreen says.

Patrick glances about. "Is that you, Mr. Farnsworth? Are you causing this? Why don't you show yourself to us? Or are you going to hide inside this doll for all of eternity?"

A sharp blast of wind whips up from the floor and encircles us. It's stiff and bitter, filled with the souls of those who died here at the hand of this monster. The breeze takes on a cloudy haze as it surrounds us in a whiplash of power. Dirt blows all around the room, and I squint to see through the particles. My hair is flying about behind me and I feel as though something wants to push me to the floor. I resist, though, fighting off the heaviness by sitting tall and holding on to Celia's and Patrick's hands.

"We're not leaving, Mr. Farnsworth!" I scream.

The floor starts shaking again, and rocks and clods of clay tumble from the walls.

"I'm scared," Becca admits.

"Don't be," Loreen tells her. "Be strong, Becca. We all have to be."

The spirits continue to circle, hands, arms, and fingers reaching out in search of—what? The bitter wind spins around us in a hurricane of pressure. The negativity level within this cave is blatant and I feel my heart will beat straight out of my chest.

Then Xander falls over again, flat this time. The earth shifts beneath him, and the air lashes around him, pulling him up off the ground in a tornado effect.

"Oh my God!" Celia exclaims. She tries to drop my hand to reach for the video camera.

"Don't break the connection," I snap.

"But this is *actual* poltergeist activity and I *have* to get it on film."

"We have to pass these spirits on," I say.

"Phillip Farnsworth, in the name of God, I pray for your trapped soul and wish you nothing but happiness and peace," Loreen says, even though we all know that the man doesn't deserve such a kind blessing.

Althea's eyes are wide, but she doesn't seem surprised at what we're witnessing. Xander rises about a foot off the floor and spins around in the air. Suddenly, the loudest noise I've ever heard in my life peals out. It's a combination of a firehouse siren and a bobcat screaming. The wailing rattles my bones and freezes my blood in place. The noise is horrendous, as if someone is being torn limb from limb.

"Leave this doll!" Loreen shouts out over the piercing howl. "Now!"

"I want to cover my ears," Becca says, tears escaping her eyes. Patrick says, "No! Hold tight."

We're all caught up in the airstream whizzing around us. The whiteness of the mist surrounding us tunnels up to the ceiling and around the room. I don't know whether to follow its path or squeeze my eyes shut from it. It's like that scene in *Raiders of the Lost Ark* when they open the Ark of the Covenant and all of the spirits soar out and melt the faces of the Nazis. I certainly don't want that to happen. I've seen enough skeletal remains for one lifetime.

A roar echoes throughout the chamber. "My house!"

"Is that you, Phillip? Show yourself if you can," I say.

The bellow increases and the walls shake again. "My house! Get out!"

Patrick looks into the swirling mist. "*You* need to get out. We are releasing you from this object. Go into the light."

"There is no light for me!" the voice growls.

Xander the Doll comes crashing to the ground and we're all tossed backwards, breaking our circle of joined hands. A flash of vibrant white explodes from the ground. The figure of a man shoots out and hangs overhead.

"Dat's the master," Althea cries.

"What? What's going on?" Celia asks, sitting up. She and Becca can't see the bedlam surrounding us.

"Loreen, you did it!" I say.

"You're free, Phillip Farnsworth. Now leave this house and go into the light," Patrick shouts.

"There is no light for me!" the voice of the figure repeats gruffly. "Damn you! Damn you for doing this!"

From the hole in the floor, black shadows slip out and envelop the space. Caped arms enclose the specter of Phillip Farnsworth and he lets out a bloodcurdling scream. A chill like I've never felt before covers me and I'm paralyzed from the waist down. Blackness overtakes the room and grasps at Farnsworth's spirit. He struggles and fights, not wanting to go, but they pull him down, down, down with them into the earth, into the dark, and the mist follows all of them into the ground in a long *hissssssssss*.

I put my hands to my mouth at the realization of what's just occurred. "Did he just . . ."

"Get pulled into hell," Patrick finishes.

"There was no light for him," Loreen says, righting herself.

"The temperature is going back to normal," Celia says. She turns to me. "We just missed something really awesome, didn't we?"

I hold on to her arm. "I'll tell you later. I don't know if I'd describe it as *awesome* though."

She shakes her head. "You psychics get to see all the cool stuff."

Shuddering, I say, "I wouldn't call it *cool* either."

I lift the now-lifeless body of Xander the Doll off the floor, dusting off the dirt. I cradle him gently in my arms and kiss him on the head. "Thanks for protecting Robert from his father's abuse. Now you're just a toy again. An old, old toy from a world long gone. You're not going to hurt anyone anymore or jinx them or curse them."

I withdraw the vial of holy water and sprinkle it on Xander's head. I hand the antique back to Celia, who takes him cautiously. Then I turn to the remaining two spirits.

"It's time for you to go now."

"I don't want no endin' like dat," Althea says in a shaky voice.

"You won't, Althea. You're special. You protected the innocent and gave your own life for them. You deserve peace."

We all circle again and pray for Althea. Loreen repeats the instructions she gave to Mr. Farnsworth. Only this time, I feel it will take her to a higher place.

"Thank y'all for sendin' love and prayers to me. All I did was love dem children. I'd a ratha the massah beat up me instead of his own. I was wrong ta curse Massah's soul and put him in dat doll. When I think a all the trouble dat was caused . . ."

"Don't, Althea, you didn't know. You believe in things that we don't necessarily understand or agree with, but you did what you thought you had to for your charges," I say.

Farah wraps her arms around her new friend. "Althea, Kendall's right. You'd known nothing but hatred in your world. You didn't cause all of those accidents or fires or mishaps. You *were* the protective nanny those children needed."

Patrick hugs me from behind, both of us needing a bit of stability for a moment.

"Call out to your family, Althea," I tell her.

"I don't reckon I can remember 'em all," she says, wringing her hands.

"Call out to Robert then."

Althea lifts her eyes. "Robert? My boy?"

"Hey, look at that," Farah says, pointing up. "It's gorgeous. So bright and warm. I see my YaYa."

"Who's that?" I ask, unable to witness what she's seeing.

"My grandmama."

"Go to her, Farah," I say with tears in my eyes.

Althea stretches her arms out. "I see muh Robert. He's wavin' to me."

The tears cloud my vision, but I know I'm witnessing something made of pure beauty. I blink extra-hard and sniff. Althea wraps her arm around Farah, and my cheerleading friend waves at me. "Tell everyone I said bye," Farah says with a great big smile. "I'll be singing in heaven with the angels. And, boy, am I going to give them a run for their money."

I laugh through my tears as Farah winks at me.

The two figures nearly blend into one and then they disappear.

I slump into Patrick's arms and he holds on firmly to keep me from falling.

Celia walks over to me with Xander the Doll. "Did they go?"

Nodding, I wipe away my tears with the back of my hand. Then I reach for Xander. She hands him to me. He's light and airy and . . . just a doll. There's a goofiness to him now, as well as in the expression on the stuffed bear with the crooked face. "I believe there's finally peace here."

Loreen places her hand on my shoulder. "We can go."

Fifteen minutes later, covered in dirt but no worse for the wear of our adventure, Loreen, Patrick, Becca, Celia, Xander the Doll, and I emerge from the secret tunnel. Mass and Patrick work at the knobs on the mantel to reverse the open-sesame we created. When the fireplace is resealed, we all look at one another.

"Man," Becca says. "That was intense."

"I'm sorry I missed it," Shelby-Nichole says sadly. "After what I dealt with at my house . . ."

"It's okay, hon. Really," I reassure her.

"What happened?" Father Mass asks.

I heave a sigh of sadness. "There are some dark stories in this town, Father. Tales that no one would believe if you told them. Ones that should be buried down deep to die with those that caused them. A nasty bit of Radisson's history was just revealed to us."

Becca looks scornful. "Yeah, but we have no real proof of

what just happened other than some EVPs, maybe something on the video; it's mainly personal experiences that happened to y'all."

"The skeptics would eat us alive," I say. "A spiritual cleansing, dark figures from below, and two souls reaching their heavenly peace." I lift my eyes to Celia's. "What happened has no basis in science, but it was real. As real as us standing here."

My friend loops her arm through mine. "I know, Kendall. I believe you."

Father Mass reaches out and tweaks Xander the Doll's arm. "What about this fellow?"

"He's just a doll, Mass," Loreen says with a grin.

"Yep, that's all he is," I agree.

Celia and I go upstairs and carefully place Xander back into his case. I blow him a kiss because I know he won't cause any further trouble. The damned soul inside him found his just reward in the underworld.

"Do we tell Mr. Pfeiffer?" Celia asks.

"Nah . . . he thinks we're a bunch of meddlesome kids. Let him keep thinking that. Things will change around here. The air in the house is already lighter. There won't be any more mischief attributed to old Xander here."

"So, we just let the legend of Xander the Doll continue," Celia states.

"Yeah, why not? Now it's a great town legend. The letters of forgiveness will keep coming in as long as the exhibit travels."

"What about correcting the history books about the Under-

ground Railroad coming through here? We owe it to history."
Celia has such passion for the subject.

"We promised Mr. Pfeiffer we wouldn't reveal any of our
findings." I reach for my friend. "It's okay, Cel. We did what we
were supposed to do."

She exhales noisily and relents. We back out of the room,
relock the door, and slip down the stairs to meet up with the
rest of the team. Becca, Patrick, and Shelby-Nichole have already packed up the equipment, so we're ready to go.

Patrick meets me at the bottom of the stairs and encircles
me in a gigantic bear hug. I cling to him wearily, as I am totally
spent.

"We done good here tonight," he whispers into my hair.

History might not ever know of our accomplishment, but
we know.

## CHAPTER TWENTY

WET SANDPAPER SWIPES ACROSS MY CHEEK and I brush it away. It returns with more vigor and verve. I smack it again. It won't stop.

*Slurp . . . slurp . . . slurp . . .*

I open my eyes to discover Buckley curled up on my chest, licking my face. I pull his furry self up into my arms and kiss the crooked gray spot on his nose over and over and over again so he knows what it feels like to be smother-loved.

"Hi, baby kitty. Who's the baby kitty? You are. Yes, you are."

He blinks at me and keeps trying to lick me with his abnormally long tongue. Natalie meows from her spot at the bottom of the bed, none too happy that her beauty rest has been interrupted. Eleanor grunts her hello before flipping upside down next to me and burying her head in the covers. There's nothing better than waking up surrounded by so much love and trust. Especially after the roller coaster I rode last night.

I'm feeling more rested this morning than I do most Sundays after I pull off an intense ghost investigation. Then again,

I didn't channel and I wasn't the one physically tossed around like poor Celia. Man, that girl's going to have some serious bruises this morning. That aside, I'm wicked proud of the work we did and how we helped Farah and Althea and released the nasty spirit of Mr. Farnsworth.

Rubbing Buckley's outstretched chin, I tell him, "I never want to deal with anything like that again. That was freaky scary. Yes, it was . . . yes, it was . . ."

He just purrs, unaware of what I handled last night. Maybe there is something to voodoo, or vodoun, as Father Mass calls it. *Something* attached the soul of Phillip Farnsworth to that doll, and he'd been making trouble for the living ever since. In the end, it was bad. Very bad. Borderline demonic, and all I know is I want no part of it. No messing around with curses or charms or dolls where spirits or souls can be stored. Yikes! No way, man. Demonology is nowhere in my past, present, or future. I can't wait to get to church today and cleanse myself in the well of Father Mass's sermon and good old Communion.

After crawling out from the cat-laden covers, I strip to my undies, pad to the bathroom, and proceed to take the longest, hottest shower in the history of all showers. I soap my hair twice with the Aveda rosemary mint shampoo, careful to get every last clod of Georgia red clay out of the follicles—was too damn tired to do it when I came home last night. I don't want *any* reminder of that dark tunnel and what happened there.

The freshly washed towel is soft on my wet skin, which is a little sore from all the climbing, crawling, and saving Celia from a sinkhole. I wrap it around me like a sarong and then drag the paddle brush through my hair. Using my forearm, I clear off the steam from the mirror.

*"Ahhhhhhhhhhhh!"*

I jump.

I scream again.

I drop the brush.

Anona stands behind me with a glower on her beautiful face.

"Don't do that to me!" I fuss. "Honestly, that's like a horror-film move, Anona."

She just stares at me, unblinking.

I turn. "What? What now?"

Her lips part and a faint smile spreads. She holds a hand out to me. "You've done well, Kendall."

"Thanks, A," I say, returning the smile.

"There is more."

"More? More what?" I don't want to go back into that under-the-fireplace tunnel full of spiders and bugs, skeletons, and God knows what else we didn't discover. I certainly never want to witness the chilling black figures of death pulling another soul into the depths of hell again. That's what it had to be. I witnessed a descent into hell, no doubt about it.

"You will hear from him," she tells me and then fades away.

I yell out at nothing. "Him who? What now? It better not be that Farnsworth guy, Anona!"

There's a knock at the bathroom door and then Mom peeks in. "Everything okay in here, Kendall?"

"Yeah, Mom," I say, retrieving my brush. "You know me . . ."

"Yeah, sweetie, I do. That's why I asked."

I stick my tongue out and then smile. Mom just winks. The door clicks shut and I stamp my foot. "Thanks a lot, Anona," I mutter.

Great; another vague ghost leaving me a coded message. I swear, when I die (at a very old age, thankyouverymuch), if I need to come back through the veil and contact someone, I'm going to speak to them in clear, concise, complete sentences, not puzzle pieces that don't fit together no matter how hard you jam them. "Ah, well . . . it is what it is."

I step out of the bathroom and head to my room. I've got some churching to do.

Right in the middle of Holy Eucharist, my cell phone starts playing the theme song from *Ghostbusters*. Why in the world did I let Celia talk me into letting that be my ring tone? I cringe as I pull the device from my purse and try to silence it. Every eye in the sanctuary shifts to me, and I turn nineteen shades of crimson and wish a sinkhole would open up and swallow me. Nah, better not wish that. It just might happen.

"Kendall, I told you to turn that blasted thing off," Mom hisses under her breath.

"Sorry," I whisper.

Father Mass stifles his mirth and continues with the service.

I click off the phone and stash it deep into the black hole that is my purse, although my psychic senses tell me it's something imperative. I mean, my friends know I go to church at this time, so they wouldn't dare call, and Patrick's not going to buzz me up now since he's still unconscious on Father Mass's couch after a long night of investigating followed by some much needed Kendall-cuddle time.

It's totally not appropriate of me to be thinking of our make-out session while in the house of the Lord, my place of respite from the long night and brushes with pure evil. I shift my attention to Father Mass.

"Beloved in the Lord: our Savior Christ, on the night before he suffered, instituted the sacrament of his body and blood as a sign and pledge of his love, for the continual remembrance of the sacrifice of his death, and for a spiritual sharing in his risen life. For in these holy mysteries we are made one with Christ, and Christ with us; we are made one body in him, and members one of another. Having in mind, therefore, his great love for us, and in obedience to his command, his church renders to Almighty God our Heavenly Father never-ending thanks for the creation of the world, for his continual providence over us, for his love for all mankind, and for the redemption of the world by our Savior Christ, who took upon himself our flesh, and humbled himself even to death on the cross, that he might make us the children of God by the power of the Holy Spirit, and exalt us to everlasting life."

It's like Father Mass is speaking directly at me, knowing I need to connect with my religion after what we observed last night. I do believe God protects me in my work. Why else would I have been given this gift if not to *truly* assist those who need me the most? Still, there's an overall sense of ickiness from our investigation that only some one-on-one time with the Almighty can cure.

Father Mass continues. "But if we are to share rightly in the celebration of those holy mysteries and be nourished by that spiritual food, we must remember the dignity of that holy sacrament. I therefore call upon you to consider how Saint Paul exhorts all persons to prepare themselves carefully before eating of that bread and drinking of that cup."

The words *holy mysteries* are emphasized by my priest and this too I feel is for my benefit. There are many mysteries in this world that many "normal" people don't see or even know about. Some things that no man is privileged to know no matter how much he tries. This is why we have faith. Faith in ourselves. Faith in our family. Faith in our friends. Faith in our beliefs.

I believe I did right last night because I had faith in Althea and faith in Farah. I also had faith in the abilities that have been given by my Creator. This is my new way of thinking. My new purpose in life that Oliver and the counselors taught me.

The usher indicates that our row can go forward for Communion. I follow Mom and Dad with Kaitlin right behind me. We walk up the aisle to the altar and kneel on the red velvet bench. Father Mass brings the cup and the bread to us. I watch as my sister takes Communion. She makes a face at the taste of the unleavened bread and then sips at the wine like it's poison. I can't help but roll my eyes at her. Such a brat.

Father Mass stops in front of me. "The body of our Lord Jesus Christ, which was given for thee, preserve thy body and soul unto everlasting life. Take and eat this in remembrance that Christ died for thee, and feed on him in thy heart by faith, with thanksgiving." He lifts the cup to my mouth and I drink down the too-too sweet wine. "The blood of our Lord Jesus Christ, which was shed for thee, preserve thy body and soul unto everlasting life. Drink this in remembrance that Christ's blood was shed for thee, and be thankful." Then he pauses and places his hand on my head. "Be thankful, Kendall, for you are blessed and you will be called to service," he whispers.

"Thank you, Father." Like I haven't already been?

My priest moves on to give my mother the sacrament and I get an itch below my skin surface telling me that there's much, much more in store for this day. Has Father Mass become psychic through osmosis by hanging with Loreen and me?

He winks my way.

Does he know something I don't know?

"You have one new message."

Oh no, please not the haunted-sandwich man—who's been quiet of late. I hope I haven't conjured him up.

"First new message, received at eleven thirty-four."

I press *1* to listen. "Hello, Kendall. This is Paige Miller. I'm the assistant to Oliver Bates. He's doing a fellowship this summer in Europe to try to solve several cold-case homicides and missing-persons cases. He's putting together a team of his former retreat attendees who he feels possess special talents that could aid him. These students will travel with him and work on the cases. If you're interested and your parents would like to speak with Oliver or me, I can be reached at . . ."

My mouth hangs open as I sit on my bed—still in my church clothes—and listen to the message for the third time. I'm by myself in the house, as Mom and Dad took Kaitlin to her soccer team's spring picnic. Not even the cats are around to shout the news to.

Am I interested? Am I *interested?* Are you frickin' kidding me? No, I'm not interested at all in going to Europe with Oliver Bates. I'm not the least bit inclined to want to get near Italy in the hopes of finding Emily's parents, my grandparents John Thomas and Anna Wynn Faulkner.

Umm . . .

Yes! Yes! Yes!

I take a deep breath, scroll to my most recent missed call on my phone, and hit Send. This has to be big if she called me on a Sunday morning to give me the news.

"Paige Miller," the kind voice at the end of the phone says.

"Hi, Ms. Miller, this is Kendall Moorehead. You called me about Oliver's Europe trip?"

"Oh, yes, Kendall," she says. "Oliver speaks very highly of you and we'd like to include you in his tour this summer, along with others from your retreat."

I listen intently as she details the itinerary—which includes a stop in Italy, *booyah!*—and what would be expected of me. I will be given a minuscule amount of information on the cases, be shown pictures of the missing or deceased, and be allowed access to some of their personal items. From that, we would try to warm up the case enough to give police clues to go on. My excitement soars like a kite on a windy beach. Then my heart plummets to my feet when Paige details the costs. Hotel and other housing will be covered by Oliver, but I would need airfare and money for food and general spending, and that just ain't gonna happen.

There's no way I can ask my parents to foot the bill for this, especially since they paid for Oliver's retreat and the plane tickets to St. Louis to see Andi Caminiti. This trip would be a total dream come true, but I just don't think we can afford it. Besides, Kaitlin's going off to soccer camp in Florida and I'm sure the parentals would like to spend some money on a nice vacation for themselves for once.

"I'll tell my parents about it, Ms. Miller. When would I need to let you know?"

"As soon as possible," she says.

"Thanks." I hang up the phone and look at the notepad where I'd jotted down Paige Miller's phone number. I scribble the details and the bottom-line price. Seeing it in writing doesn't make it any more affordable.

I sulk away from the phone and throw myself across the bed. I'm all ready to set the table for a gigamonic pity party when Patrick rings the front doorbell. What? I know it's him without even looking. I bound down the stairs, the notepad still dangling from my hand, and let him in. He scoops me into his arms and swings me around and around.

"You got the call too," he says, excited.

"Yeah, I did. So?"

He puts me down. "So, we're going to Europe, babe!"

"With what? My looks?" I'm way too snarky for my own good.

"Your looks will take you a lot farther than Europe. They'll take you to the moon."

Great. Patrick got the call too. I mean, *awesome* that he got the call, but I so don't want him going to Europe without me. All those gorgeous French girls and Italian models. Oy on the vey. I glance down at the figure scrawled in my excited, shaky handwriting and feel my spirit slope further into depression.

He reaches for my hand and grips it in his. "I'm not going without you."

"That's so sweet, Patrick. There's no way, though, that I'm letting you give up a mondo opportunity like this because of me." I pause and then ask, "How are you going to afford it?"

"I have money saved from not taking diving trips and from

the job I had when I lived in Tampa," he says, trying to cheer me up. "Just talk to your parents. Or Loreen. Maybe you can do some extra hours at her store to get some of the money."

I stare at my hand where it joins Patrick's. "I don't know. Maybe."

Why can't I catch a break?

"Come on, babe. I've got to leave in a few hours. Let's go to a movie or get some ice cream to celebrate. We will be doing this together."

The thought of a sugar-free Moose Tracks milk shake lifts my spirits. I drop the notepad on the kitchen counter and grab my car keys, following Patrick out the back door.

When I return, after a bit of a tearful goodbye—or rather "see you next weekend"—hug and kiss to my boyfriend, I find Mom and Dad sitting at the kitchen table going through their monthly bills.

They're doing this to see if they can pay for Europe for me. It's written all over their faces. I glance down and see a bill from the hospital—from my surgery—and another from the lab that's doing the DNA testing for us. I've totally cost them enough money for one lifetime.

"There's cold chicken and deviled eggs in the fridge from the picnic, sweetie," Mom says nonchalantly.

"I'm not really hungry," I say. Couldn't have been the twenty-ounce milk shake I sucked down in five slurps. Nope, not at all.

Dad adjusts his eyeglasses and calls out to me. "Is there anything you want to discuss with us, Kendall?"

"Like what, Dad?"

"Oh, I don't know. Maybe an invitation to join Oliver Bates in Europe this summer?"

I kick at the kitchen island with my foot and don't meet my dad's gaze. "It's no big deal, Dad. You know . . . whatever."

"Now, Kendall, don't act like Kaitlin," Mom snaps. "This is not 'whatever.'"

Turning to them, I say, "You guys have already spent enough on me. Look at all of these bills because of *me*. Maybe another summer . . . another lifetime."

"Sweetie," Dad starts. "Your mom and I are looking over our finances to see if it's possible, okay?"

I raise a brow at them. "Seriously?"

"We can't promise anything," Mom says. "But we'll try."

I run to the table and hug them both. "Thanks, you guys."

## CHAPTER TWENTY-ONE

AFTER PATRICK LEAVES, I spend the rest of the afternoon working on the Civil War paper that's due tomorrow. Nothing like waiting until the last moment, huh? Good thing I can type extra-fast and can get the whole thing done in no time.

> *The Underground Railroad was a system of covert routes and safe houses used by black slaves in the United States to flee to free states or farther north to Canada. Many were aided by abolitionists who were compassionate about their cause. Started in the early nineteenth century, the Underground Railroad helped nearly one hundred thousand slaves escape; however, U.S. census figures account for only six thousand.*

My fingers fly over the keyboard, logging dates, names, and historical facts and figures. I cover the Fugitive Slave Law of 1793; William Still, the father of the Underground Railroad, who helped as many as sixty slaves a month to their freedom; Harriet Tubman, who made thirteen trips to the South and back to aid people; terminology along the route; and the route itself. I scroll through the document, and I'm quite proud that I've been able to pull it all together in the eleventh hour like this.

Of course, I purposely leave out the part about there being a station in Radisson, Georgia, under Farnsworth House. There's the secret tunnel under the fireplace, but I really have no proof of what occurred there other than what I learned from Althea. Sure, archaeologists and historians could dig through that passageway and probably make great findings to add to Radisson's already rich history. But that's up to them, not me. My job was to help those spirits into the light—and now it's to write a paper that will wow Mr. Rorek and get me an A in his class.

I do feel the need to editorialize a bit at the end, based on my experience with Althea. I stress in my paper the horrors of slavery as a whole and how our nation can never return to such atrocities. I also praise those who had the courage to leave their families behind for the freedom they sought. The unsung heroes are those who aided the slaves, oftentimes hiding them in their homes or farms or businesses, sometimes sacrificing their own lives for what was right and just.

*The lesson we learn from the War Between the States and the valiant effort of those who worked in the Underground Railroad is that we must never allow history to repeat itself. That you should treat others*

*as you want to be treated. As Thomas Jefferson wrote*
*in our own Declaration of Independence: "We hold*
*these truths to be self-evident, that all men are*
*created equal." Let that be the lesson of the*
*Underground Railroad.*

"There," I say, happy to be done. If I don't get a good grade on this, Mr. Rorek's been drinking way too much coffee and it's damaged his brain cells.

I hit the Print button, and my BlackBerry rings. I dive for it, thinking it's Patrick telling me he got home safely. It's Rebecca, though.

"Hey, Becca."

"Hey, I wanted to check on you and see how you are after the investigation."

"I'm actually okay," I tell her. "Not nearly as exhausted as I usually am after a spirit crossing. Then again, Loreen and Patrick were there to help."

"Good. I was worried about you."

"No worries. Have you looked over any of the footage?"

"Yeah. A lot of mists I can't explain, some black shadows crossing the screen, and a whole hell of a lot of EVPs that are just a little too creepy to listen to so fresh off the investigation."

"That's okay. We'll get to them in due time. I know it's hard for you and Cel to follow along when so much is going on, like it did last night."

I know she's smiling into the phone. "I trust y'all will tell us if we're in danger or anything."

"You know I will!" There's an underlying sense of giddiness from my friend that she's not revealing to me—something about a journey . . . a competition. It's not totally clear, so I push her for information. "So, a trip and a contest?"

Becca laughs. "You're good, Kendall. Yeah, I've actually been bouncing off the walls today. It's been hard to concentrate with such amazing news."

She's going to tell me *she's* going to Europe too.

"I got picked to go to Paris this summer for the DanceFest Parade, which is this huge four-day street party where DJs from all over the world get to spin their music. There are vendors and tattoo artists and palm readers and food and—oh my God, you name it. And they want me!"

I cram down my jealousy and sing her praises. "Of course they want you. You're the best damn DJ around. No one spins like you, Becca!"

"I'm beside myself," she says with a happy sigh.

"How did you get invited?"

"Some guy on the committee saw my Facebook page and clicked on some of my mixes. He said they're trying to get younger DJs involved. There's a scholarship for the under-twenty DJs who go and spin. Can you imagine if I can win actual college money?"

"How are you paying for it?"

"Dad's letting me use some of the savings my grandmother left me. Other than that, I'm going to backpack and stay at youth hostels and just . . . live."

"That is fantastic, Becca! I'm super-juiced for you." And I am. It's not a lie. I just wish I could go with Oliver Bates's crew or with Becca.

"You have to come, Kendall."

I snort. "Yeah, right. And do what?"

"Set up a booth. Do tarot readings, fortunes, anything. You'll make a ton of money."

"I don't think so."

Becca makes fun of me. "Just consider it. We could have an amazing summer. Oh, Dragon's here. Gotta go!"

"Love ya; mean it," I say and then click off the phone.

Great, my second offer to go to Europe in one day and I just don't see it happening. Even my psychic senses are laughing at the idea. It would be amazing to work with Oliver again, or to make some euros reading cards on the Seine. I rub at my nose, which is blazing with itchiness. Maybe Patrick's right: if I worked at Loreen's store every day after school, I could raise some serious dough. I crawl under my bed and retrieve the Aldo box that holds my best sparkly summer sandals. Underneath the tissue is my savings envelope, which has exactly . . . twenty, forty, sixty, eighty, eighty-five, eighty-six, eighty-seven dollars. That won't even get me a cab to the airport.

I scrub at my nose again. *Why* is it itching like all get-out?

Grandma Ethel always said when your nose itched you were going to have company.

Right. Who else is coming to tell me he or she is going to Europe?

Sunday evening, I pick at the spaghetti on my plate, pushing the noodles and sauce from side to side. The modest amount I ate is sitting in my stomach like a boulder. I'm trying not to pout, really I am, but a heaping serving of disappointment is the topping to my pasta.

"I just don't see how we can afford it, sweetie," Dad had said at the start of dinner. Now, he watches me with a long face. I know he feels like shit having to squash something this major for me. I understand, though, that times are tough, there's college to save for, and, again, they've spent a lot of money on me recently.

To ease the tension, Dad switches on CNN to watch the disaster reports, government crises, and political scandals du jour.

The front doorbell rings, and Kaitlin starts to bolt.

"Don't you dare, young lady," Mom says. "Eat your dinner. Your father will see who it is."

Dad puts down his fork and disappears into the hallway.

"It's probably Daisy or Penny bringing me the book of cheat codes to use," my sister says.

"Cheat codes? Great." I turn to Mom. "What is the point

of letting her play all of those video games if she's going to cheat?"

"It's not cheating, Kendall," Kaitlin whines. "It shows you how to get more lives or more stones and stuff and powers to fight the bad guys."

"Right—cheating," I say firmly. "Thus the reason they call the book *chea*—"

My mouth falls open midsentence when I see the visitor Dad has brought into the house.

Andi Caminiti stands in my dining room in designer jeans, a loose red tank top, and a large purse slung over her left shoulder. How did I not see this coming? Stupid psychic abilities. They've been dormant all day because I've been working on my history project.

"H-h-hi, Ms. Caminiti," I manage to stutter out.

"I'm so sorry to have interrupted your dinner," she says sweetly. "And it's Andi."

Mom stands and pulls a dining-room chair up between her and me. "Won't you please join us? David makes fabulous spaghetti sauce."

Andi holds up her hand. "No, that's nice of you." She reaches into her purse and pulls out a large manila envelope, slightly bent at one corner. "I should have called you when this arrived in the mail yesterday. I just couldn't bring myself to open it alone. I closed the shop, packed a few things, got in my SUV, and, well, here I am."

"Oh my goodness," Mom says. "Please, come sit and let me

get you something to eat and drink. How long a drive was that?"

"It's really fine, Sarah. Maybe in a little bit."

My heart is churning like a fan switched to high. Andi's is too. The energy humming off her tells me she's as eager for these results as I am. She *wants* me to be her brother's daughter. And I want her to be my aunt. I envision all the things we'll do together as we get to know each other and I learn every detail of Andy Caminiti's life. I push back from my chair and walk over to her. She reaches her hand out to capture mine and gives it a squeeze. "Shall we do this together?" she asks.

Words aren't a possibility for me right now, so I simply nod and smile.

We walk hand in hand to the formal living room, the one no one ever dares enter—not even the cats—because you don't want to mess up the curtains, smoosh the cushions, or get dirt on the pristine rug. However, this occasion calls for the most special room in the house, and Mom leads the way. She flicks on the antique hurricane lamp, flooding the space with warmth and light. Andi and I take a seat on the white couch with the large envelope balanced on our knees.

"Well?" she asks.

Without thinking twice, I flip it over and rip into it. I tug out the sea of papers and speed-read past the cover letter. My eyes blur when I see pages of charts with numbers, letters, and general gobbledygook all over them.

"Mom," I beg, "I can't make it out."

Mom the nurse takes the papers from me and retrieves her reading glasses from the top of her head. Her eyes scan the pages as she flips one, then two, then three of them. A few moments later, Mom removes the glasses, and her eyes are shiny with fresh tears.

"What? Tell me, please."

Andi pleads too. "Yes, Sarah, what does it say?"

Mom smiles at Andi and then at me. "Kendall, baby. You've found your father."

# CHAPTER TWENTY-TWO

"WH-WH-WHAT?" I squeak out.

Mom blinks and then says, "Andrew Caminiti is your biological father."

Hot, hot tears fill my eyes as my brain tries to reason and comprehend the words. Emotions line up one by one to spill over me in a waterfall of relief, joy, happiness, confusion, loss ... all at once. Even though I know who my biological parents are, I will never *know* them. A young man and woman so in love, yet they died tragically in a December car crash. I crumple a bit on the couch as the sensations filling my soul get the best of me.

"Oh, Kendall," Andi says. I glance up to see her arms open wide, inviting me into her family, into her heart. "I'm so sorry for doubting you and for being so rude when you first came to my gallery."

We hug tightly, clinging to each other as the tears overcome us both. Looking over Andi's shoulder, I see my mother is weeping as well. She's not upset, though. She's happy for me.

Overjoyed, in fact. The nurse who helped me into this world and then took me on as her own when my parents died. I love her so much, and I mouth the words at her.

Mom blows a kiss at me as Dad comes to comfort her.

"I don't blame you for thinking I was wack," I say to Andi. "It was quite a story I came in with, but I was led to you through my visions."

Andi wipes the salty water off her cheek. "I should have known after taking one look at you that you were Andy's. You have his eyes."

"Yours too," I add with a smile.

She hugs me again. "I have a niece!"

"I have an aunt!"

My mom's tears continue, so I go to her. Hugging her with all of my might, I thank her for everything: my life, my home, helping me find out who I really am.

She squeezes me back. "I want nothing but happiness for you, Kendall."

"You're still my mommy," I say softly and she kisses me on top of my head. We stand like that for a moment and then Dad joins the hug-dom.

I push back and take a deep breath. "Okay, well—wow, what a day!"

"David, let's leave these two to talk more. Andi, I'll make up the pullout in the den for you. Please make yourself at home. You're family now."

Her hazel eyes shine up at Mom. "Thank you, Sarah."

We sit back on the couch and face each other. My aunt. I'm facing my aunt. My father's twin sister.

Reaching into her bag, Andi pulls out a small accordion file and then tugs out a thick photo album that's cracked at the binding. "I brought these in anticipation of the results. This one is a family album filled with pictures of Andy and me when we were growing up. I thought you'd want to see your father at all ages." She flips to the back to show a photo of the two of them in dark navy robes and mortarboards graduating from high school. "He was a really good-looking guy. All the girls thought so."

My own eyes gaze back at me from the handsome young man on the page. Yes, I do have his eyes. Hazel and warm and smiling so brightly at the future he had ahead of him. I well up again, thinking of all he could have done with his life, the family I could have had with him and Emily, things that would never come to be. But I have to be grateful for the opportunities I've been given, despite my troubled entry into the world. Things could have been sooooooo much worse for me. I could have died along with my parents and never have known the Mooreheads, Grandma Ethel, all of my friends, Loreen, Father Mass, and especially Jason and Patrick.

"Here, this is yours for as long as you'd like it," Andi says to me.

I run my hands over the worn leather of the family album.

Slowly, I flip through the plastic-protected pages that show my father's life: a tiny bundle coming home from the hospital; a little boy riding his Big Wheel; a teenager in his Boy Scout uniform; a young man setting off to college. I'm sure I'll spend several hours poring over these pictures and trying to get any place-memory that may be attached to them.

My curiosity is piqued by the accordion file. For some reason, my nostrils are filled with the smell of rubber. Industrial rubber. Totally an odd thing to be picking up right now as Andi opens the folder.

"What's all that?" They look like the stock-report pages we studied in economics.

"When Andy disappeared, we put the money from his trust fund in a stock account, in case he came back. Over the years, we've donated some of it to charities for tax purposes, but I never imagined that he'd have an heir to give this to."

She hands me the stacked reports, oozing with dollar signs. "I don't understand."

"This is Andy's inheritance from our parents. My grandfather founded the Caminiti Tire empire in St. Louis and passed it on to my father. After Dad died, when we were thirteen, Mom sold the business and set up funds for both Andy and me. I used mine to get my gallery going and just monitored Andy's all these years. Now it's yours, Kendall."

"My father came from money?" Like the Celia Nichols kind of money? My eyes dart across the report. It's not a fortune, but it's *muy* substantial. I mean, like paying-for-college substantial. Money that's been earning interest over the last seventeen years. *Whoa, Nelly!*

I try to calm my excitement with a deep breath. "Can I do anything I want with this?"

"Sure," Andi says. "What were you thinking? A new car?"

I snicker. "Actually, no, I have a great car. I was thinking of going to Europe this summer with it. You know that TV show *Ethereal Evidence?*"

"Oh, sure, the one with the psychic guy with the mustache. He's amazing."

"Well, I know him and he wants me to help him out with some cases in Europe this summer, only I didn't really have the money for the trip."

Andi points to the bank report. "Now you do."

I call Mom and Dad back into the room to tell them of my newfound wealth. "May I use some of it to go with Oliver and the other kids this summer?"

My parents exchange glances, and then Dad says, "It's your money, Kendall. You can do what you'd like."

"I'd like to go to Europe." I turn to my aunt. "And I'd love it if you came with me. Can you? You know, to chaperone? We can get to know each other better and you can tell me all about my dad."

Tears sprout from her eyes again and a smile shimmers out. "I'd love to, Kendall."

We hug each other again. Suddenly, I feel that my world is righted and back on its axis.

———

Monday's a horrendously busy day at school. I turn in my Civil War report, help out with the yearbook, and fill Celia, Becca, and Shelby-Nichole in on everything that happened on Sunday. That was only yesterday? Holy cow!

"So, I can't believe that just like that, you're an heiress," Celia says as we're leaving school. This is the third time she's uttered this phrase today.

"Not an heiress like you, Cel." But enough.

"Any way I can go on this European adventure with you?" Celia asks, so innocently.

"Seriously? Your parents will let you?"

"Duh. Have AmEx, will travel."

"Of course! Let me call Oliver's assistant and tell her that we work together. With your artistic skills, you can definitely help on the cases if Patrick and I pick something up."

"That would be super-cool. I'll totally pay my way and I won't be a burden or get in your hair."

"I'm not worried about that at all," I say with a laugh.

She adds, "We can go to Paris too, and see Becca in her competition."

"Oh, you know it." What a difference twenty-four hours makes in a person's life.

We stop in front of the Radisson Historical Society. The gloom and despair that once encircled this structure seem to be gone. My psychic headache isn't alerting me to anything evil or dangerous; it's just a beautiful old house among the oaks now.

"Well, we're here," Celia says. "Are you okay with this?"

"Absolutely. Let's go."

Mr. Pfeiffer sighs when he sees us but reluctantly lets us in. We follow him through the hallway and into the great room, where Celia and I sit opposite from him on the couches. He seems different today, not as ready to combat us as before. I sense that his nerves have eased and he's not going to explode from the tension in his head. Slowly, I begin to relay all that happened Saturday night, including telling him about the secret passageway under the fireplace. He needs to know everything, even if the town doesn't.

"We cleansed the manor of the bad spirit hanging around and helped some slave spirits pass into the light. You shouldn't be frightened of the house anymore, Mr. Pfeiffer," I assure him.

He begins to tremble, and the walls of his defenses crumble right before me. "I always knew there was something here. Something watching me. I've been tripped on the stairs, pushed, had what little hair I have left pulled, and had a lamp thrown at me. I had my duty to the Farnsworth family, though." He wrings his hands. "I do thank you. Today has been different for me here. I don't feel like I'm being watched and I'm not hearing the moans and groans from the walls that I usually experience."

Concerned, I reach out to him. "You should have told us these things, Mr. Pfeiffer, instead of fighting us."

"I didn't . . . didn't want to believe."

Celia speaks up. "As a historian, you have an excellent chance to do more research, open up this house, and really let the public delve into this part of Radisson's olden times."

"You're right, of course. I'll see what I can do."

"And, Mr. Pfeiffer?"

"Yes, Kendall."

"Xander the Doll is okay now. He's just . . . a doll again. You can take him out of the case and display him wherever you want."

His eyes glance at me knowingly and he nods. "I'm sorry for my previous impatience, but I do thank you for changing the atmosphere here. I'll see what I can do to get it opened to the public."

I stand and offer him my hand. "Thanks for your help and for letting us investigate."

He shakes my hand and smiles.

Celia and I walk out. I have one more visit I want to make.

We cross town and go out to the old cemetery where I first saw the parade of Union troops. Now, on this blue-skied sunny day, a soft breeze blows through the trees with not a whisper of times gone by. Instead, there's peace in the green valley and I have a bundle of flowers to deliver to someone special.

I go over the river and down to the back portion of the cemetery, then I walk up to the freshly dug plot and kneel in front of the marble headstone that reads:

FARAH DARLIETTE LEWIS
BELOVED DAUGHTER
WHO NOW SINGS WITH THE ANGELS

I set the bouquet of pink spray roses at the foot of her headstone. Others have left things: pictures, stuffed animals, and musical trinkets. She was definitely loved, and the loss of her in our community will be felt for a while.

"Miss you, Farah. Rest in peace."

The only answer is the rustle of the leaves as the gentle wind trips through the tree branches. Farah's not here to answer. She's found her final rest and truly *is* singing with the angels. For a moment, I can almost hear her voice floating through the air.

It's hard to accept when someone dies so young, like Farah, and like my parents, Emily and Andy. That life is stopped in its tracks. Dreams, hopes, and plans are no more. What's left is a marker like this one and the memory of their presence. With my parents, though, their families didn't even have that. It's the main reason I want to find the Faulkners. With Andy's parents both deceased, the Faulkners are the key to knowing everything about my birth mother and how I may have gotten these abilities. Sadly, we lose loved ones—or those we never had a chance to love—but everything happens for a reason. It's not for me to understand or question; it's for me to continue on my path, helping others, using my gifts as best I can.

And that's exactly what I'll do.

## Chapter Twenty-three

"No, you did'unt!" I shout two weeks later when I see the long, white stretch limo stop in front of my house on Saturday night. I release the curtain of my bedroom and turn one last time to check my appearance in the mirror. Mom helped me with my makeup—a little MAC shininess in the creases of my eyes—and I tried out a new curling iron to make finger curls all over my head. Man, that took, like, two hours, given how much hair I have. But it looks awesome. Like I went to the salon and paid a fortune for a custom do.

"What is it?" Celia asks, returning from the bathroom. She looks breathtakingly amazing with her freshly washed and curled short hair and the sleek black cocktail dress that shows off her miles and miles of long, slender legs. The girl could totally be a model if she set her mind to it.

"The boys rented a limo."

"How cliché," she says, peeking through the curtains. "Holy crap! It's the Hummer limo. That must have cost them a fortune. For what, a six-mile ride to the hotel ballroom?"

I smack her on the arm. "It's one of those rites-of-passage things, remember."

The doorbell rings and Mom calls out, "Girls, your dates are here."

Celia wobbles a bit on her two-inch heels. "Careful there, Cel!" I say.

"Oh my God, these things are impossible. How do women wear these every day?"

"Because they're pretty," I say, glancing down at my own sparkly high heels.

"Can't I just wear flip-flops? Or better yet, my Timberland boots?"

I laugh so hard that it threatens to smear my makeup. "Dude, you should totally start a fashion trend. Cocktail dress and mountain boots."

She staggers again, catching herself at the top of the banister.

"You look gorgeous, Cel. Just walk slowly."

I let her take the stairs first, bending down a little to catch the look on Clay's face. Cel could be on any runway in Milan or Paris, the way she looks tonight. Clay's eyes literally twinkle and he smiles broadly as he holds his hand out to her. He's wearing a traditional black tux with spit-shined shoes. Awww, they are so cute together.

"This is for you," he says to her almost shyly. He slips a corsage of red roses onto her wrist and they move out of my sight.

Okay, I'm up.

I hold on to the railing as I maneuver the soft, shifting light blue dress in front of me. The hem hits right above the knees, a full satin skirt covered with netting that has rhinestones scattered about. The camisole bodice fits nicely to my body and has shimmers of light and dark blue beading on it. I step down the stairs one at a time, careful not to take a tumble. That would be so grace-like of me to do that.

*I see your feet,* Patrick says.

*I see yours.* He's wearing his black high-top Chuck Taylor All-Stars.

*Can't wait to see the rest of you.*

*Here I come.*

A gasp escapes from my guy as I walk down the final steps.

His smile is wide, vivid, and ever so approving. "You look like a princess," he says.

"That's good, right?" I tease. Yep, this dress is a far cry from my jeans, T-shirts, and ghost-hunting ensembles. I do sort of feel like royalty.

My prince is wearing a black suit over a Hawaiian-print shirt in sea foam green. His shaggy hair has been combed into place over his forehead, and his brown eyes shine from beneath his gorgeous black lashes. The look totally works for him and we're going to be adorable together at the prom.

"Oh, Kendall, sweetie," Mom says, her hand to her heart. "Beautiful. Just beautiful."

Dad snaps a pic with his digital, almost blinding me with

the flash. "Give me some warning next time, Dad," I say with a giggle.

Patrick hands me a lovely corsage of baby's breath, lilies, and white spray roses. He really does know what I like.

*It's 'cause I know your every thought.*

I elbow him a little as I slide the corsage into place on my arm.

"Let me get a group picture," Dad says, motioning to Celia and Clay.

The four of us stand together at the base of the stairs as Dad snaps away. One of Patrick and me. One of Clay and Celia. One of just the girls. One of just the guys. One of the four of us. *Click, click, click.*

"Okay, Dad, that's enough," I say, unable to see anything but balls of color blinding my vision.

In that moment, Anona appears. I wince involuntarily, afraid that she has bad news for me. Or that our spiritual cleansing of Xander the Doll didn't work and there's trouble in Radisson that we need to attend to instead of celebrating our prom.

Instead, she beams at me, her dark eyes dancing.

In my head, I ask her, *Is everything okay?*

*Fine. Everything's fine. I was sent to tell you that they're very proud of you.*

*Who is?*

*Your parents.*

*I know, can't you tell? Mom's crying and Dad won't stop Nikoning me.*

*No, Kendall, your birth parents.*

*Emily and Andy? They're together?*

*Yes. They're happy and at peace. And so very proud of the woman you've become.*

*Can I talk to them? Will they come see me?*

Anona places her hands together, nods, and disappears.

My chest squeezes as an overpowering ray of love shines on me. Something Anona spread to me, or perhaps a gift from my parents together in heaven. Either way, I *do* feel loved—by them in heaven, by my earthly parents, by my friends, and by Patrick.

He lays his hand on my arm and slides it down to engulf my small hand in his larger one.

*I do love you, Kendall.*

*I love you too, Patrick.*

"Are we ready to go or what?" Clay asks.

"Let's do it!" Celia shouts.

"Have fun!" Mom calls out as we make our way across the front porch, down the steps, and to the waiting Hummer limo.

"You guys are insane renting this," I say.

"It's okay," Clay says. "My dad got us a steal of a deal."

"And we have an amazing surprise for you too," Patrick says with the cheesiest of grins.

Celia and I do our best to climb into the monstrosity of a vehicle in the most ladylike manner possible. We sit facing each other, and the driver takes off. Sparkling cider and crystal champagne flutes sit in a console nearby, so Clay pours us each a glass.

Patrick takes his but makes a quick phone call before drinking. "We're on our way," he says. I'm unable to pick up who he's talking to because he's totally blocking his thoughts from me.

*Brat!*

*Patience!*

"To great friends," Clay says, holding his glass up.

"To us!" I say.

"To a great prom night," Patrick chimes in.

Celia says, *"L'chaim!"*

We all stop and stare.

"It means 'to life' in Hebrew," she explains. "What? Taylor's not the only one who knows other languages."

Loves me my Celia. We clink our glasses and drain the sweet, bubbling liquid.

"We're almost there," Patrick says mischievously. He reaches over and switches the button to open the sunroof. It hums along as it opens.

"Stand up," Patrick says, doing it himself.

"Are you kidding me? After spending most of the afternoon on my hair?"

"Come on, Kendall. We're only going like five miles per hour."

I shake my head. "Okay, fine. But if my hair looks bad in the pics, I'm gonna beat you." We laugh together.

"You too, Celia," Clay says.

She has no problem stretching upward and leaning out over the roof. "What a beautiful night! What are we waiting for?"

"You'll see," Patrick says as he holds my hand.

We clear the square and turn down Ferris Street, on our way to the hotel where the prom is. All of a sudden, I get the sense of something sparkly in my immediate future. No! Not a ring—hello, only seventeen.

My intuition is right on the nose. On the dark stretch of road, I suddenly see sparks of white light—actually, white, silver, and gold fireworks volcanoing in six cones on each side, to a height of about ten feet, popping and crackling in a festival of excitement. It's an amazing display showering over us as we pass slowly in the limo. It's like being surrounded by millions of tiny stars that are shining only for us. And at the end, I see Loreen and Father Mass on either side of the road with lighters and morning glory sparklers in their hands, igniting the last cone.

They both wave. "Have a great time tonight!" Loreen shouts.

We signal back and then I turn to Patrick. "That was amazing."

"You're amazing," he says and leans in to kiss me. A soft, warm kiss that melts every bit of me from the top of my curled hair to my sparkly evening shoes.

This truly is a night I'll never forget.

I don't know how it can get any better.

The hotel ballroom is decorated to the hilt in dark blue streamers with silver stars on them and white and silver balloons all over the room. White trellises line the walls with weaves of colorful flowers that look and smell amazing.

I struggle for breath as I take in the beauty of it all.

"Smile," the photographer says to Patrick and me. Patrick is positioned behind me, his hands on my waist, in front of a backdrop of a dark starry sky.

*Click, click, click.* Instant memories frozen in time for all to see.

A bounty of food is laid out for us, as well as frothy pink punch, sodas, and more sparkling cider. The live band is playing hits from the '80s, which the chaperones seem to really dig. Becca mocks putting her finger in her mouth to gag when the Bee Gees sound out. They should have hired her to spin some Trance, House, or good Dubstep.

However, an old George Michael song, "Careless Whisper," begins to play and Patrick pulls me out onto the dance floor and into his arms. I close my eyes and lay my head on his shoulder as he moves us around to the slow beat of the music. I'm safe. I'm secure. I'm loved. And I have an exciting future. Father Mass was right. There's more in store for me and I *am* truly blessed.

The cute guy dancing with me is proof of that.

"May I have your attention?" Kyle Kadish says into the microphone when the song is over. "We have a very special presentation this evening." He glances off to the side. "Mr. and Mrs. Lewis?"

Farah's parents step forward. The junior and senior classes explode in applause, and Mrs. Lewis begins to get weepy and motions us to stop.

"Thank y'all for your love of our daughter," Mr. Lewis says. "We want to thank you all for caring about our Farah and sending cards and flowers to us. It means more than we can ever express. And we wanted to give back something to the student body of RHS, a place Farah loved so much. Singing and cheerleading were her life. We want everyone to remember her school spirit, as well as her own lovely one, for all time."

Kyle helps Mr. Lewis unveil a large frame. I feel my heart beating furiously in my chest over the display in front of me. It's Farah's actual white RHS cheerleading uniform—the one she had gone home to retrieve—framed and matted, with a picture of her in the corner smiling out at everyone with her green eyes.

Everyone claps heartily, and I know mine aren't the only moist eyes in the crowd.

"And now," Kyle says, "a moment of silence for our friend Farah. May she rest in peace."

The silence in the ballroom is admirable, yet I open my eyes and glance about. No sign of a spirit. No presence here at all. I did help Farah pass on to her eternal rest. Because of her, Althea did too. Everything truly does happen for a reason. It may take us time to figure it out, but that's what life's all about.

I blow a kiss to the heavens for Farah, and then add two more: one for Emily, one for Andy. *My parents.*

"Thank you," Kyle says. "Without further ado, here is our prom queen and court." The gathered crowd begins to giggle and chatter and buzz with excitement. Kyle takes a white envelope from inside his jacket and opens it. "This year's prom princesses are . . ."

"I'll gag if Courtney's crowned queen," Celia whispers next to me.

"Shhh," I say, trying not to laugh.

Kyle's voice booms through the ballroom. "Stephanie Crawford . . ."

Stephanie shrieks and then dashes to the stage. Kyle loops a princess banner over her red formal.

"Next prom princess is Courtney Langdon."

"That's a shocker!" Becca says from behind me.

Courtney feigns a happy smile, but I can tell she was expecting the crown and not just a glittered sash. Still, she waves at the crowd in her skin-tight silver-sequined dress.

"And the final princess," Kyle says, "is . . . Kendall Moorehead."

*Ex-squeeeeeeeze me?* "What? Me?"

"Oh my God, Kendall!" Celia shouts. "That is the coolest thing ever!"

Patrick hugs, kisses, then releases me, scooching me on my way to the stage.

My hands are shaking like a California quake and I'm sure

my feet aren't touching the ground. Me? Seriously? Did he read that right? I'm psychic, but I didn't see that one coming at all. Not one inkling.

Up on the stage, I join Stephanie and Courtney and accept the sparkling banner from Kyle.

Wow, if these two are princesses, who in the world will be the queen?

I stand blinking at my fellow students who voted me onto the court. Me, the new girl. The freak. The psychic. The ghost girl. Staring at the sash around me, I finally feel like I fit in. Like I'm just Kendall.

"The moment you've been waiting for," Kyle announces. "This year's prom queen—rightly so—is Farah Lewis."

Everyone bursts into applause again, and I join in. Of course. Farah. That's a no-brainer.

Mr. and Mrs. Lewis hug each other on the side, still crying, only this time with joy over the love the student body has shown for their daughter.

Courtney, Stephanie, and I take the rhinestone crown and set it on the corner of the uniform portrait.

"Miss you, Farah," Courtney whispers.

"Me too," Stephanie echoes.

"Me three."

The band begins to play our school's alma mater as an air of sadness and nostalgia passes over the group. We all join in to sing together, a tribute to our fallen—but not forgotten—friend. So many people pass in and out of our lives; some will never know how they touched us. Footprints stay on our hearts, and we're better off having known them. It's all part of the discovery of life. Who we are. Where we fit. What our purpose is.

I smile out at Cel, Becca, and Patrick. Definitely imprints on my soul.

The song goes into the second verse, everyone doing his best to sing to our heavenly friend. Somehow, I don't think Farah would like our pitch.

But she'd definitely appreciate the efforts.

# EPILOGUE

"MORE BISCUITS COMING OUT!" Mom shouts to our filled-to-capacity dining room the morning after prom.

I'm still numb that I was an actual prom princess. The satin banner now hangs on the corner of my mirror in my room as a reminder that I've found a new home after all.

Cel and Becca slept over here with me—although there wasn't much snoozing, mostly giggling, girl talk, and dishing on our guys. Mom and Dad have let me host a huge breakfast for everyone on Sunday morning. Celia, Clay, Courtney, Ryan, Jim, Sean, Kyle, Stephanie, Becca, Dragon, Shelby-Nichole, Patrick, and I gather around, munching on homemade frittatas, fresh-cut fruit, grits—a Southern staple I've learned to love with some salt and butter—crispy bacon, bagels, cream cheese, and lox. Mom really outdid herself. She even squeezed fresh oranges to make juice for us. Now that's love.

Father Mass and Loreen are here helping out my parents, drinking coffee, and making sure no one's glass gets empty.

I've never seen Courtney Langdon eat this much food. "You've simply got to give me the recipe for this frittata, Mrs.

Moorehead," she says, singing the praises of my mom's cooking.

A goofy smile spreads across my face as I look around the room at the friends I've made in such a short time. And now, I have an extended family with Aunt Andi and my continued quest to find Emily's parents. Thanks to the wonderful generosity of Oliver Bates, I'm going to get to go to Europe to further develop my psychic abilities, help families in distress, and possibly locate John Thomas and Anna Wynn Faulkner. It'll be the best summer evah, and oh yeah, I'll get to spend lots and lots and lots of time with Patrick too.

Could life *be* any better?

The phone rings off in the distance, and Dad calls me over to it.

"This is Kendall."

"Miss Ghost Huntress, this is James Pendergrass."

Ummm . . . errr . . . oh, crappity-crap! It's the haunted-sandwich man!

"Yes, sir, how can I help you?" I feel horrible that with everything that's been going on, I've totally blown off this guy and his problems. Who am I to say his sandwich isn't haunted? Although I do believe in the heart of my psychic abilities that this man needs mental help, not ghost busters.

"Well, Miss Moorehead, the haunted sandwich stole my car and totaled it. My insurance company won't pay for it because the sandwich wasn't on my policy."

Oh. My. God.

"I won't be needing any further help, though," he continues, "because the wreck seemed to have destroyed the haunted sandwich forever."

I cover the receiver to muffle my giggle. I just shake my head.

Yup. This is my life.

I finish with the call in time to hear the front doorbell ring. Mom scuttles off to answer it. Before the door opens, though, I'm blinded by a vision of someone with beautiful blond hair, straight white teeth, and a happy smile, standing next to another person who's frowning and scowling with ultra-blue eyes. I'm so enthralled by the turnout here today that I don't exactly add two and two together in my psychic mind.

I hear Mom welcome the new guests, but I don't dwell on it as I add more cantaloupe chunks onto my plate next to my toasted sesame bagel.

Then it happens.

My heart stops for a moment and then restarts like a ticking time bomb.

"Well, look who's here!" Mom shouts out.

I don't have to look because I know. Without a doubt.

A shrilling scream of happiness is followed by "Taaaaaaaaaaaaylor!"

My friend Taylor Tillson rushes into the dining room in all her blondness, hugging and air-kissing people on her way to me.

"Kendall!" She hugs me tightly and I do my best to squeeze back in my surprised state. "I just got in late last night. Mom is out of rehab and I told Dad that I wanted to come back to Radisson to help her out."

"That's fantastic," I say, so happy to see her perky face.

"Where's Patrick?" she asks with a cheeky grin. "I can't wait to meet him."

I reach into the crowd and tug him away from a convo with Dragon about rice rockets. "Patrick, this is—"

"Taylor Tillson," he says with a grin. "Kendall's told me all about you."

Tears fill my eyes as I watch my friend flit about the room as if she never left. "She's back," I murmur. Maybe she can go to Europe with us this summer. Of course, if Taylor's here in town, does that mean . . .

Before I can finish the thought, blue eyes slice over me as Jason follows in his sister's wake. Jim and Sean high-five him, but his eyes never leave mine. I'll admit that my body physically reacts with a pounding in my chest when I see him move through the room. Then the blue orbs shift to where mine and Patrick's fingers are entwined.

*That's Jason Tillson*, Patrick says to me.

I gulp hard, knowing I don't need to respond.

Jason, still tall and gorgeous and able to make my treacherous heart take a roller-coaster dip, steps forward like an alpha dog. He sizes me up in one glance and then does the same to my boyfriend.

Patrick bows up a bit too, moving in front of me slightly to mark his territory.

"Hey, Jase," I manage to squeak out, trying to take the initiative, be the grownup, and be nice.

His face softens and his eyes shine happily. I can tell he wants to reach for me, but I must have that "don't go there" look on my face. Instead, he just smiles that award-winning modelesque grin that won me over in the first place so many months—and so much drama—ago.

Jason parts his lips and then says, ever so lazily, like nothing's changed between us, "Hey, Kendall. I'm back."

All I can think is: *Oh, crap.*

*To be continued . . .*

# DISCLAIMER

The thoughts and feelings described by Kendall and her friends are typical of those experienced by young people awakening to sensitive or psychic abilities.

Many of the events and situations encountered by Kendall and her team of paranormal investigators are based on events reported by real ghost hunters. Also, the equipment described in the book is standard in the field.

However, if you are a young person experiencing psychic phenomena, talk to an adult. And while real paranormal investigation is an exciting, interesting field, it is also a serious, sometimes even dangerous, undertaking. While I hope you are entertained by the Ghost Huntresses, please know that it's recommended that young people not attempt the investigative techniques described here without proper adult supervision.

# Sources

The idea for Xander the Doll is loosely based on the Key West legend of Robert the Doll. For more information, check out www.robertthedoll.org.

Holy Eucharist information from justus.anglican.org.

Information on the Underground Railroad from en.wikipedia.org/wiki/Underground_Railroad.